Jezebel
Born to be...
That girl.

Jezebel2

Lilly Buchanan

Published by Lilly Buchanan, 2024.

JEZEBEL2

First edition. May 4, 2024.

ISBN: 979-8215286326

Written by Lilly Buchanan.

Dedication

To all of the women who didn't have to be Jezebel.

To My brothers, Robert, Mark , Darby and Jason. Anything is possible!

Jezebel
Lilly Buchanan

"Such beauty was never seen in all the land"

King Ethbaal

"This part is ALL about Me written by ME! "Jezebel

My Father, Ethbaal, the King, said that the day I was born, the Sunset early, ashamed to be surpassed by my beauty.

Born in Phoenicia (now known to you as Lebanon) located to Israel's north...I was a child of ultimate privilege.

My father was the King, and being an only child gave me certain advantages that other girls obviously did not possess. Anything I could ever dream of, was mine for the asking. I was the spoiled apple of my Father's eye.

My earliest childhood memory is being invited to a birthday party for one of the children whose father was employed by my father. I took her a gift of silver hair combs, as was appropriate for a child of five.

It was a grand affair. Too grand; I remember being insulted at the opulence of the party. There were so many guests, the cake was huge, and the number of presents was staggering.

I remember my father commenting out loud that he must be paying her father too much money if he could afford such a massive display of celebration. It was almost as lavish as one of my parties!

I will admit to being jealous; especially when her big gift from her parents turned out to be a stunning brown and white miniature horse, with a solid white mane and a bright pink bow around her neck.

At this particular time, miniature animals were a mystery. No one in our area had seen such a small, full-grown horse! It was absolutely beautiful and the way the sun's rays hit the horse's mane made it appear to sparkle.

I looked at my father, and said firmly "I want that horse!", he smiled and told me he would have me one by the next day. I stood my ground and said, "No, I want THAT horse."

Long story short by the end of the party, the little horse went home with us. The birthday girl cried enormous amounts of pitiful tears but I didn't care. I had to have that horse. My father did not do it in a way to embarrass the child's father. He offered him a ridiculous amount of money for the animal and probably a promotion. Her own father sold her out, so I felt no remorse about the situation. In my world, I always got what I wanted so this day would be no exception. Everyone else seemed to live in my world because I allowed it.

I had finer clothes than anyone I knew, more golden bracelets, and more beautiful possessions. Any and all slight suggestions were embraced by my father, the King. My life starting from the crib was lavish and delicious.

I did not have a mother in the traditional sense; we did not have the typical mother-daughter relationship. She gave me birth then was removed from my life when I was very young. I was beautiful and apparently, she was not. I don't remember what she looked like however, my father used to say she looked like that would happen if a pig had mated with a horse cart. He said she was tall and broad but with a long narrow face. He mentioned it every time I asked, just to hear me laugh.

I wondered why he married her if he felt this way and many years later I found out that she had been heir to copious amounts of property and wealth, which of course became my father's immediately upon their marriage. She was an only child and when her father died, she was given the inheritance as a son would receive. Her uncles (her father's brothers) were furious however, that is exactly as her father demanded it. He adored his only daughter and wanted to secure a future for her. Kings and their sons were falling over each other trying to snag my mother's fortune, I meant, her hand, but her father was adamant that she marry someone who would cherish her. It took years searching for the right King for her but he finally found my father and arranged the marriage.

It was said my parents appeared to be ridiculously happy until my grandfather died.

I was taken away from my mother when I was very young. I cannot remember the exact circumstances; it seems like one day I remember her being there and then the next she was not. I can remember being told repeatedly that my mother was not safe to be around and that she didn't like children. I am sure I can remember her screaming but either I learned not to hear it or she quit screaming. I am not sure which.

My father was my hero, so I cannot imagine him doing anything to infuriate her so. I remember feeling anxious when I would hear her screaming at him. My father did not tolerate her. At the age of 8, I overheard a conversation between several servants...they were explaining to a new servant, who was curious about my mother, that my father claimed one night that my mother tried to kill him in his sleep. He woke up gasping for air, and that was when he realized something was covering his face. He fought his way out of it and discovered my mother trying to smother him in his sleep by sitting on his head with a pillow tied to her buttocks!

He couldn't publicly put her away and risk her uncle's trying to invalidate their marriage and take her currency and properties back. So, he basically imprisoned her in our Castle.

They also said my father was terrified she would try to harm me as she tried to him. So instead of allowing me to be influenced by her, he hired others in her place to raise me.

The largest and strongest guards were hired to protect us from her and

the finest nurses were hired to meet my every need. He explained he had placed guards throughout the castle for our safety and for hers. He said he was afraid she might try to harm herself if left unattended.

The few times I was around her, she never acknowledged me or even pretended to recognize me. She always seems to be in a trance or something. I remember her wearing long flowing dresses with a head covering so I could not see her eyes. I grew up not knowing her. But don't feel sorry for me. I had a great childhood as you will read. My father, MY Father, The King, My hero, always went above and beyond for me in every aspect of my life. He loved me so much he even went as far as protecting me from the very one who gave me birth.

No one mentioned my mother. She never even had visitors. If someone did visit, my father would tell them she was not receiving visitors and change the subject. It was just accepted that it was a topic no longer to be discussed. I was allowed free reign of the castle, except in the section my mother was being held.

I found out early that I had some power, servants would stop and bow every time they saw me.

This made me smile knowing that I, a little princess, had the power to make someone do something just by seeing me. I loved to make people bring me things simply because I could!

My Father and I had a never-ending date. Once a month we would put on our best royal clothing and go to the garden for a tea party or luncheon. I loved this time with him and he loved it too. He would hold me up in the air and swing me in the air. He would allow me to put my feet on his and we would dance. These are such fond memories of my childhood!

On my 10th birthday, my father gave me a huge party. All of his friends came with glorious gifts! Except for the family that I took the horse from. A messenger arrived to tell us that apparently all of the family had gotten a serious case of food poisoning the night before the party and was too sick to possibly attend.

I didn't care if they came or not. They mattered not at all to me as long as they sent a gift. And they did send gifts; beautiful ivory hair combs, ruby and gold bracelets, and a stunning gray and white Mare.

The horse was beautiful but I gave it away to an ugly young girl at the party. She looked charming with the ivory combs in her hair and ruby and gold bracelets on her arms, riding that Mare home with her father leading the way. See, even I knew not to accept gifts from people who snubbed my father's party.

One man that Father was not entirely friendly with, brought me 3 medium-sized brown, puppies. He assured us that they were safe and loyal pets. I was not a fan of these animals but I refused to show any fear of them in front of all of the guest. I remember, as I walked cautiously towards them, two of them ran and jumped on me knocking me down and the other one started to growl as he started coming towards me, as to attack me! The crowd all gasped at the same time, and instantly the guards swooped in and tossed the three beast and the guests who brought them, out on their rears. All of them yelping (including the guest) as they departed. It troubled me very badly and it upset my father immensely that I was distressed. He raised his arms and ended the party early telling everyone to simply leave their gifts and go. When I realized everyone was going home, I begged him to stop them. I was not ready for the party to end! Father called everyone back and the party continued as if nothing had happened.

It turned out to be a magnificent event! All of the gifts were top quality, fitting for a Princess like me. It took hours to open all the presents and for the recorder to list each present and giver, so they could be sent acknowledgment notes. It was a stately event! My father let me pick which gifts I wanted to keep and ones I rejected were left for any children that attended.

It was an indirect, no knowing my father as I do it was a direct slap in the face of anyone who didn't bring a magnificent gift.

My father always checked the list to see who brought what and he would remember the offenders in his own way. Call it what you will, but my father demanded and always received, the best for me.

Before bed that night my father came in to check on me. He knew I had hurt my knee when the pups knocked me down. As soon as I saw him, I told him, "father I don't like dogs, even small ones. They are too bouncy and that one was even mean. The way he growled at me, I thought he was going to bite me!" My father sat down next to me and held me to him. "My sweet baby girl, My princess, you were very brave today! I am so sorry that happened to you. You will never have to worry about dogs again! I promise!"

Authors Note: This is a promise that not even the great King Ahab would be able to keep. Please read to the end of the book.

As the years went by my nurses groomed me in ways of life, how to care for my hair, how to be healthy, and make good choices with food. Beautiful women were hired to teach me all I needed to know about being beautiful and how to take care of my body. I was pampered and given every type of spa treatment known to man, to keep my skin clear, my teeth white, my hair shining. They taught me how to walk properly and dance and carry myself as the true beauty that I had become. Father was very much involved in the supervision of my care and if he even suspected one of the nurses or women were jealous of me or disapproved of me, he would have them beaten and escorted quickly from the Castle.

I was the little Queen at our Castle. In a time when women were not considered valuable, except to have babies and cook, I would rise above them all. My father had no sons, I was his heir, and his heartbeat.

I attended all functions with my father as his companion. Even the ones that no other children were in attendance. Eventually, I hosted gatherings at our home for my father's friends and acquaintances. I was always by his side. When he traveled, I was there with him. Those who knew me would always boast to my father how beautiful I was and that none other compared to me. I had a rare natural beauty that transcended any need for even color for my lips. Even I loved to catch a glimpse of myself in the calm water pools. It was amazing to me how my large round eyes were the color of chocolate and my nose had a small little curve on the end of it. Even my ears were pretty and dainty. I loved how my hair was the color of honey with just a hint of dark streaks in it. I had an exotic look that probably only Princesses get. I had my father's features and he said I had his mother's eyes! In a country full of dark-haired women, I stood out.

I may have been just 12 years old but I was a full-grown woman in my own mind.

As I slid my hand down the curve of my side to my hips; like I saw the female dancers do, a smile would always come to my lips and I would think no wonder people are so nice to me. I truly am as beautiful as they say.

I could watch myself in the reflection glasses for hours. Father had those special-looking glasses made for every room so I could be free to move about the house and see myself. He loved to watch me admire myself. He would laugh so loud; it just made him happy.

My father bent over backward to make sure I had a need for nothing in my life. I had the best of everything that could be eaten, worn, or used! The special perfume was made just for me! No one in all the land would smell as marvelous as me. My nose was very sensitive to bad smells. I just couldn't stand any bad smells. My father had the stables moved further away from the castle because the occasional wind would bring the smell to my nose and offend me. After a traveling messenger's body odor offended my nose so badly, Father decreed that all visitors to the castle had to be bathed and clean before being allowed an audience with the King.

Scented oils were rubbed into my feet and hands, wonderful lotions on my body and magical conditioners in my hair. I had massages almost every day of the week if I wanted them. I loved the feel of my back and legs being rubbed! I simply could not fall asleep properly without my back being rubbed.

Father always allowed me to determine our nightly menu. He was so happy just to have dinner with me. If I decided I wanted only potatoes five nights in a week he would allow it simply because he wanted to please me. He would surprise me with exotic chocolates several times a month as he knew I loved them so much!

At the age of 13, I had my own transportation cart and servants. I decided I no longer required nurses as I was now a woman.

I had recently walked in on a situation where the main nurse Sabrina was telling the other nurses how spoiled and ungrateful, I was. They were all giggling at her demonstration of my behavior.

Having their full attention, she began to mock me in a loud, high squeaky voice... "Rub my back Sabrina, kiss my feet Sabrina. Feed me some grapes Sabrina, wipe my behind Sabrina" the nurses began to laugh harder. Sabrina put one hand on her hip and began to prance around the room, presumably acting like me. "I am a Princess and you are all beggars. You should be proud to care for such a raving beauty and stop breathing the air I breathe you peasants!" The other women collapsed into uncontrolled laughter. I couldn't take any more, I clapped my hands loudly and yelled "Stop" everyone froze with terror as they realized I was there amongst them. I smile sweetly and said, "What fun you are all having at my expense.

Of course, ALL of you are now dismissed from my service! I am sure my father will be very interested in knowing how dreadfully you have spoken of me. Now get out of my sight!"

They ran from the Castle in fear of my Father, and did not return to try and explain their behavior. When Father returned home, I told him what had happened and that I had fired all the nurses. He smiled at me and said, "Well done my precious. No one is welcome here that does not adore you as I do. You are my prized possession and if they cannot treat you as the priceless jewel you are, they shall not be in our sight, much less get money from us! I shall hire you some companions to come and be with you during the day and I shall find the best service workers for your facials and massages." he said.

That night father allowed me to have wine with my dinner, as he just could not refuse me anything.

Over the next couple of years father brought in some teachers to instruct me on ways of the world. Politics and religion were big topics of discussion. I was to be taught these things so I would be aware of them. It was really rather boring to me. Father always sat in on the tutorials so he could hear what views were being presented to me. Of course, he would always interrupt the teachers and tell them they were wrong or right and make his own opinion known on every subject.

I was instructed on policies of the land and learned about countries that were enemies and allies. It was interesting at times, and boring most times, but it was my education.

I want to let you in on a big secret, I have never told anyone! We (My Father and I) personally do not follow any religious belief in our hearts. Our entire country follows the god "Baal." Many countries worshipped Baal and hundreds of other gods. Some even believed in one God which we thought was ridiculous! However, to put up a unified front, my Father and our entire household are followers of Baal, but between the two of us and only us, I admit we did not believe in any god. Being the governing face of authority, we tried to unify our citizens by "Being as one". The citizens had to bring sacrifices of the finest meats and vegetables to the gods, which we ate! They brought silver and gold and treasures to the worship place, which we confiscated and used for our own purpose. Our great wealth was increased by donations and by giving gifts to Baal. We received and kept the gifts. Father assured me there was no real gods and that this was a way to control the ignorant masses and it was also the key to our financial security. However, during my studies I did find out some interesting information about other religions in the lands. The idea of them captured my attention during the lessons.

My father realized my peaked interest and told me that he just wanted me to learn about the existence of other religions so I would be aware what was going on in other lands so I could understand how the people think.

"If you can find out what drives men to do the things they do, you will find the source of their strengths or their weakness" father told me one night at dinner

"The people need to trust their leaders and then leave the leading to the leaders. If not, there is discord within the country. Too many choices confuse the masses. It is always our job to convince the community that we are taking care of everything for their best interest. Without order there is chaos." Father used to say and I agreed with him.

Of course, I didn't know enough to disagree with him. In my opinion, his idea of good leadership was that the citizens put forth 150% of the effort and we just agree to be adored and honored by them. Father seemed to have everything under his control.

One area that he taught me to appreciate was his military. He demanded his Army be loyal to him in all areas. No exceptions.

My father made sure the armies were fed well and paid regularly. Defectors or even slanders were executed immediately upon the finding that they had been disloyal. Father did not want one bad attitude to turn the entire force against him. o his type of justice was usually swift. I admired that my father was a man of action.

Men and women arrived and taught me how to run a household. I was taught how to read and write and I was very good with numbers. I became skilled at inventory, counting how many horses were in the stables, how much we paid for each animal, the cost to feed them and their care, how many groceries we used in the house, the food cost, and how much we paid the servants and guards.

One day I was feeling completely overwhelmed. I started complaining about all the learning I was having to do. "Is there a reason for all of this learning father? My brain is so tired! Do all girls have to learn these things?"

"No all-girls do not have the honor and privilege of getting to learn these things. Normally this wisdom is specific to sons. Almost all daughters are allowed to learn is how to cook, clean, and spit out babies. I do not want you to ever feel ignorant my daughter. I never want you to depend on anyone for correct information or well-being. Knowledge is power my precious. I am equipping you for "power," You were made for higher stations my dear." my father said with a smile.

Soon I was making major decisions concerning our household budget. Father was very pleased with me.

"You have such a wonderful ability to pay attention to details Jezebel!" Father commented one morning after reviewing my recent decisions concerning the castle.

I had cut the servants meals to twice a day instead of three times a day. There was no sense in feeding them a full meal at night if they were going to their homes for the evening. They could darn well provide their own dinner. I dismissed three bread makers. There were originally seven.

I explained that I demanded the same service only better from the remaining staff or they could find employment elsewhere. I fired 2 stable boys that found time to wrestle in the hay instead of doing their work. I saw them with my own eyes when I walked about to see how they spent their time. The remaining staff was put on notice that I was watching them and for them to remember they were there to serve and be productive.

I fired the aging gardeners for younger men that worked for less pay and I let the full-time seamstress go. Telling her I would call her if I needed her. There was no reason for her to be "on staff" 24 hours a day.

Satisfied that I had learned about religion and politics and running a household, Father reduced my studies and let me return to beauty treatments and relaxation.

He had a high regard for relaxation techniques.

"Life can be stressful my dear so we must learn how to control anxiety and stress or it will cause sickness in our body," he said with a smile as he enjoyed his massage.

The lady giving him the massage was kind of pretty and I did not like the look on her face as she gave him obvious pleasure with her strong hands. Father always insisted the females remove their shirts so the fabrics they wore never touched his body. He said their fabrics broke his concentration on the medical benefit of the massage.

It was logical that their breasts would brush his skin periodically. I watched in boredom until he sent me to my room for my foot massage. I held back just a few minutes to watch from the door as my father rolled over and took the servant girl and positioned her on top of him, she started to moan as she rocked on him and it upset me so I went quickly to my room.

I was no longer in the mood for a massage and dismissed the women waiting for me. What I had just witnessed upset me!

I had a bad dream and could not go back to sleep. I dreamed my father had remarried and the new Queen was hateful and mean to me. She looked a lot like that woman that gave him that unique massage!

I got up from my bed and went immediately to my father's room. His guard informed me that he was sleeping soundly and I could hear he was snoring loudly.

I just kept wondering around the house until I arrived at my mother's door. The guard posted outside the door snapped to attention when he realized I was there. "How are things here?" I asked. He answered that everything was in order.

"I want to see her," I said.

"Miss, I don't think that is a good idea" the guard answered. I couldn't help but notice he looked terrified! Looking back now I know he didn't have a choice about being terrified!

My father would have him killed for letting me see my mother, or I could have had him killed for denying me entrance.

"I don't recall asking what you think. Now open that door!"

He looked to his left and to his right as for an escape route then he looked directly at me and stood his ground, saying,

"I have specific orders from your father, The King, that you are not allowed here, for your safety Miss. Now please, for both of our sakes, go back to bed. Your mother is a dangerous woman, you and your father could be harmed or worse should she escape."

I could hear chains dragging across the floor from inside the room and a woman's voice repeating over and over, "Who is there? Has someone come to save me?" "Who is there?" "Has someone come to save me?"

It was unnerving to hear her voice, so I decided to leave because I chose to, not because that big jerk guard wanted me to.

The next morning at breakfast I spoke to my father. "I'm old enough now. I want to meet her."

My father's eyes bugged out of his face as he jumped to his feet and said "Precious No! I mean...Absolutely not! She is a wild, deranged woman. I cannot allow this meeting to happen. I forbid it! I have spent your life protecting you, I cannot allow this."

He was unyielding and for the first time in my life, my Father had told me No. I was shocked and offended.

I went to my room to sulk while my father made immediate arrangements to send my mother away from the Castle. This was new territory for my father and I. He had never disappointed me or refused me anything! It hurt my feelings terribly and I felt a disappointment and heaviness in my chest that I had never known before.

I happened to look out the window as my mother was quickly whisked away on a travel cart. She was smaller than I thought she would be. I always thought she was a huge woman, but she was not. She looked confused but eagerly boarded the travel cart. She looked nothing like my father had described. She did not look like a pig, nor was she ugly. When she turned to look back, I realized at that moment that she looked like... me. The very image. Her hands were chained with a small chain and her feet were in a soft shoe. Her hair was long and flowing. Her eyes were as big as mine and full of sadness. It was uncanny. It was like looking in a mirror. She and I could have been sisters. She was beautiful.

Later that afternoon I walked back to the room she had lived in for most of my life. There were chains attached to the floor that allowed her freedom to walk in a small area. There were no shackles on her bed but there were chains attached to the wall. I do not know what the need for those were.

There was a small window facing the garden, a clean chamber pot, candles sitting on candle holders, a child's doll, a handheld fan, a bottle of perfume, a silver pitcher and cup, some fresh flowers in a vase, two shawls, a pillow, perfumed lotion, a blanket and a pair of house shoes. I wondered why these various items were left behind and why were they in the room of a dangerous and deranged woman.

I met with my father for dinner. I sat quietly throughout the meal, picking at my food, and then I asked him where he had her taken to. He looked grey, almost ill, "I have sent her to live in a country farm house where she will be taken care of and cannot hurt herself or anyone else. Precious I am so deeply sorry if I hurt your feelings. Your safety and happiness are my uttermost concern. You must know that sweet daughter!"

I smiled at him, knowing in my heart he had now hurt me and denied me what I wanted. I will now be on the lookout for hurt from any man. For if my own father can hurt me and deny me, then how easy would it be for any other man to do?

I had uncovered something about my father that day that had hurt me deeply. I discovered that my father was not a Superior being, but a mortal man. A real, live man who is capable of doing anything for love, money, or anything that fancied him and the fact was, he had trained me to be just like him. It was as if a layer of hero had been pulled back, where a mere man was revealed.

In the next few days my father had called the seamstress back to come and measure me for new gowns and he commissioned a famous painter to come and paint my perfect likeness. "I will throw a party and have everyone come and admire your beautiful portraits. Would you like that dear?" father said, trying to coax me out of the strange mood I had been in.

I smiled weakly and told him that would be nice, then I asked to be excused. He shook his head yes and sadly watched me walk out of the dining room.

My father sent for a doctor to find out what was wrong with me. He explained to the doctor I had been very withdrawn and sad, even moody. When the doctor arrived, I had developed cramps and he and his nurse explained that I was getting my flow as women called it.

The doctor said it was a woman's situation and it would resolve itself.

He allowed his nurse to sit and explain to me about how all women have the flow, how long it might last, and what to do when it happens. She brought in a female servant to explain more details.

She taught me ways to try and bring comfort to my body, warm compresses to my stomach, and rest as much as possible, some suggest exercise, others suggest eating dessert, and others said drinking hot chocolate made their moods lighter. I was very upset this could happen to me but as the doctor stated it happened to all women. He said it was a sign that my body could now make babies. This opened a new discussion of where babies come from. It didn't sound very appealing. I knew that pagan sex was rampant in our country, but I always thought that was just the people acting like animals. Father had encouraged pagan sex in honor of Ba'al. He thought it was funny but the people who followed Ba'al embraced it as an act of worship. I was disgusted by them and never paid them any attention when we would leave the castle.

My father was relieved that it was nothing serious wrong with me and that my sadness should subside when the time was over.

I will always believe the shock of my father denying me access to my Mother caused this to happen to me. I had been a major part of the workings of the Castle from the beginning and he was deliberately excluding me from this one important area. He was treating me like a baby. It enraged me!

I sent the confused seamstress away when she came to measure me for new gowns. I hissed like a snake, "DO NOT come back here until I call for you.

Do you understand?" Her face was pale and tired but she whispered, "yes Miss" bowed and slowly backed out of the room.

I stormed out knowing full well my father had sent for her.

Father felt like I needed a distraction so he decided to travel and find some companions for me. He could have sent for them but he probably just wanted to get away from my madness for a while. That was fine by me, I didn't wish his company right now anyway. I didn't want anyone's company. I took my meals in my room and sulked for a week.

After about 8 days I began to feel like myself again, the flow had stopped, the bloating reduced, the pain of cramps stopped and I felt like I started living again.

I did not like the flow and all the horrors that came with it. If only I could discover a way to stop it! I am sure every man in the world would be grateful to me! I had to laugh thinking of my poor father running for the carriage as if to escape me and my bad attitude!

The seamstress came willingly when I summoned her and measured me for lavish gowns. She was very happy and pretended that nothing was amiss in our last visit.

The portrayal of Jezebel

A famous painter came to visit the castle. The King was not home and although she should not have been allowed to interview him by herself, Jezebel chose to. He was of medium build, handsome with wiry brown hair, and seductive brown eyes. As Jezebel entered the room, she could see she took his breath away, this made her smile.

"Madam!" he exclaimed "Miss" she corrected. He took her hand and kissed it gently. "I am Onligh, the master painter. You are a stunning young lady.

Will I be doing your likeness?"

She said "Perhaps" and his eyes lit up.

"This is great news! I love to create portraits of beautiful, in your case beyond belief beautiful young women" she smiled and released his hand. She supposed he had gotten so overwhelmed at the sight of her, he forgot to release her. She enjoyed his passionate attitude!

"My father tells me you are famous, known throughout the land for your painting talent"

He smiled and held up his hands showing them to the Princess palms up. "I have the ability in these hands to make ugly women look appealing, old fat women to look young and trim, skinny girls to appear fuller, but my heart to Ba'al I have never seen the likes of you in my life. Pure Perfection! And I consider myself to be a well-traveled man, having seen it all."

Jezebel stifled a giggle. He was flirting with her so boldly but she was actually enjoying it. She stood there looking at him and he slowly smiled. Jezebel spoke "...your heart to Ba'al, hmm? Are you a believer?" He moved closer to her and said "I would believe in any god that allows me to have a woman sexually anytime I want her, in any position, any day or night. He can get the glory as long as I get the woman." Jezebel laughed out loud. "You are either very brave or very stupid sir. My father would have you executed just for being in this room with me unescorted much less openly flirting with me so vulgarly."

Onligh said "I only speak the truth. All of the women fall madly in love with me because of my many talents, and I break their hearts when I leave."

"Why do they fall in love with you?" she asked quizzically.

"Because I make them fall in love with me. I find a tiny dot of fire in them and I bring it to the surface as a roaring inferno. They would do anything for me because I bring them enthusiasm, passion, and excitement! My house is filled with gold and rubies and diamonds; gifts from satisfied yet miserable women who yearn for my touch."

Jezebel's cheeks were blushing at his suggestions and it caused Onligh to laugh. "Why do their hearts break?" she asked cautiously.

He smiled slyly and said "Because they fall hopelessly in love with me and it devastates them when I leave. They want me to stay longer and keep making them feel like goddesses." Fearing he had said too much, he spoke softly "My dear, I shall charge your father only half of my normal fee because the pleasure of you will be enough compensation for me."

He walked around her and lightly ran his hand across her waist and down her back stopping just above her buttocks.

Jezebel could feel his breath on her neck and the goose bumps on her skin. She closed her eyes as to drink in the delicious, yet dangerous feelings, and then she stepped away from him and said,

"You may leave now. I will tell my father I am not ready to have my portrait made. I will have him send for a true Master Painter when I am ready. I prefer to do business with proper professionals who let their amazing talents speak for themselves...not act as rabid dogs in heat. If you ever even think of touching a royals robe again, remember that your fingers you value so much, can be ripped from your hands. I am sure my father, the King, would have them, starting with removing your fingernails, and your fingers would follow one by one."

She stormed out of the room and left him standing there unnerved with his mouth hanging wide open. Jezebel couldn't help but smile as she watched him leave from the window.

Onligh was leaving hastily as the King might arrive shortly, and he was still shaking his head in disbelief. He always won the ladies, old and young, but this one, this woman was a hard-hearted woman. As if the threat had returned to his mind, he held up his hands to look at them and shuddered before entering his carriage.

"He thought he had captured a little lamb but was sent away by a tigress instead," Jezebel thought out loud, and laughed to herself.

"No man will ever have power over me!" Jezebel said to herself.

Later that evening over dinner, when questioned by her father, Jezebel told him that the painter was very immature and that he just rubbed her the wrong way.

"I didn't like his eyes. He had shifty eyes that didn't appear to be honest. He had a way of making me feel well, uncomfortable. So, I sent him away. He was not a good fit to our home or family. And besides that father, I believe his hand to be shaking when he left!" The King just nodded his head in approval, and said "Well you are a good judge of character my dear. It is just odd I have heard so many wonderful things about his talent."

Jezebel thought back for a second then said "He may be talented Father, but no man can be as good as he thinks he is!" They shared a laugh.

The King didn't quite get the entire joke but was so thankful that Jezebel seemed to be back to her old self again. It was good to hear her laugh.

Over the next several years the King had several young ladies sent to the castle to sit with, visit, or just entertain Jezebel. Most days she ignored them. She didn't like any of them. They were either immature, or too formal, either way not a good fit for her companion wise. They were full of useless information, the latest gossip, the latest fashions, the latest love affairs, the newest vendors in the market, dismissed servants from other households. Jezebel was bored to death with the sight of them.

She suggests they find ways to entertain themselves around the castle and leave her alone. After repeated attempts to befriend her, they finally obliged her. Her Father realized this and decided he and Jezebel would do some traveling. He felt that she must still be sad and maybe needed a change of scenery.

In the months to come Jezebel and her father traveled to visit with the surrounding countries. Its only purpose was to distract Jezebel from the episode with her mother and hopefully cure her sadness. Of course, everyone assumed King Ethbaal was looking to marry her off. She was coming into the marrying age. Massive celebrations were held in their honor and almost all the Kings expressed interest in Jezebel becoming their daughter in law or wife.

Egypt put on the largest, grandest shows attempting to win favor with King Ethbaal and Jezebel.

Entire productions were planned out for her enjoyment, gifts were so large that they had to be sent home immediately as there was no room to contain them as they traveled.

Jezebel did enjoy this time with her father, but she had absolutely no desire to marry Pharoah's that already had wives and concubines. Her political inspirations were so much higher on her priority list, than clawing her way to the top of the wife chain. While Egypt was interesting and fun, she was glad to leave that country. She had to admit the views were beautiful but she was seeking a kingdom of her own. Her Father was not ready to part with her company, he knew he had prepared her to be a Queen, knowledgeable and strong but he was not ready to release her to marriage. Jezebel had not expressed any great desire to be married either. To his knowledge, she had never even looked at a man like she desired him or was even remotely interested in any man.

The king reflected on all the parties he had thrown over the years and no one man seemed to catch Jezebel's eye, never did she inquire of anyone. A feeling of guilt came over him. "I adore my daughter so much. Will there ever be a man good enough for her? A man that will love and admire her more than I do?" He sighed deeply. It would have to be a man who understands her strong will and can allow her some leeway.

Most of the surrounding countries had very young men who were to be king or very old kings who already had many wives. None were appealing to Jezebel in a marital situation. "She must have the perfect match," her father thought to himself. "Only the best for my daughter". He scratched his head for a minute and wondered how many fathers had said that about their daughters.

The last kingdom they went to visit was that of King Ahab. He was a lot older than Jezebel, possibly 18 years older, and very free-spirited. Immediately he fell head over heels in love with Jezebel. It was rather funny how he humbled himself to her service. He ran to pour her wine instead of allowing the servants, he prepared her dinner plate, serving the meats himself. He nearly tripped running to pick up her napkin that had slipped from her lap! This was out of the ordinary for any king to do!

Everyone was laughing behind his back that he was making such a fool out of himself over this young Princess, but he made no excuses, he was in love.

Jezebel's Father explained to him that he was not interested in making a marriage for her yet and King Ahab said he would wait until her father agreed it was time. He begged her father not to offer her to another.

"Name your price and I will pay it. It is my destiny to have your exquisite daughter as my wife!"

Israel, the country was beautiful. Of all the areas they had visited, this was the most fertile land and fields of growing food. All of the livestock looked fat and the people were loyal to a fault. It was even beautiful when it rained, a rainbow came out so big it took up most of the sky ending right at the gate of the castle.

The castle was huge and so spectacular. Jezebel was impressed with its massiveness and the well-thought-out gardens that were throughout the Kingdom. The King had even called his Army officials to put on a demonstration in her honor. It was a remarkable sight to see!

King Ahab asked Jezebel in person for her hand in marriage however, she smiled and said she was honored but would have to think about it and discuss it with her father of course.

King Ethbaal appeared noncommittal but all it did was fuel the fire of King Ahab. He sent massive portions of his wealth as good faith binders so that her Father would approve of the union. King Ahab spent many hours behind closed doors trying to convince Jezebel's Father how he would love and adore her for eternity. King Ethbaal tried to explain that Jezebel was not a romantic woman, but a logical woman. She was the kind of woman that felt why send her bundles of roses that will die when you can plant her a rose garden and she will have roses forever. This made King Ahab happy to learn this about her. "And she will not settle for being anyone's little woman, she is one to be involved in every aspect. That is the secret of keeping her happy, to involve her. She is very direct with her speech and not shy to tell anyone how she feels. You would have to learn her ways, her likes and dislikes. She is my only child and I have provided only the best for her." said Jezebel's Father to King Ahab. "Of course," King Ahab said blissfully, "All I have is at her disposal, what is mine is hers, completely!" King Ethbaal told him that Jezebel would send him an answer when she was ready.

King Ethbaal considered his future son-in-law. He was not even average-looking, rather plain. He was at least 18 years older than her, rail thin, and sort of feminine in his manners. He seemed undistracted by the running of his castle, perhaps he was disorganized. Jezebel would resolve that issue!

Jezebel knew she was not physically attracted to him yet she felt this would probably be the King she would choose to marry. His army was large and had great potential, and his castle was massive and properly equipped. She knew his kingdom needed better leadership, and she was prepared to be that leader. After all, she had been trained by the best. Her Father was a man of pride and a man of his word.

Jezebel assumed that this king, Ahab, could be "controlled" by a few inconvenient nights between the sheets and sweet words. Yes, she was sure this was the King she would rule. Umm, marry, she would marry this king. Then she laughed to herself at her word choices!

Her Father and Jezebel discussed the marital arrangement in detail for months. She agreed she wanted to do this. He also felt like Jezebel would be a better leader of the kingdom instead of just being a baby-making machine for a younger king. "You need to have an heir and a few other children to secure your position; however, your knowledge, abilities, and ambition, will be a great asset to your husband!" her father said. "And" he added "His kingdom is merry. You need more fun in your life my daughter."

Jezebel smiled as if her father had told a joke that was not funny.

They knew that King Ahab was weak-minded and careless in his judgments and rulings. He was too unconcerned with his servants, staff, and countrymen. They basically did as they pleased and he didn't bother with them. In most ways the kingdom just kind of ran itself, which was not normal to Jezebel. She wanted, no, needed, control and demanded the respect that came with running a kingdom.

Jezebel and her father were in agreement that the countrymen were generous to their king but the people also needed guidance and leadership. They would never accept Jezebel as a leader, so she would have to use her ability to pour knowledge and good advice into the ear of the King and to make him understand his place in the world. He was just a man and she would provide the tools to make him appear to be a great leader. Jezebel's Father asked her to wait for 3 months before agreeing to the marriage.

After 3 months Jezebel sent word to King Ahab, he may court her. When she sent her answer to King Ahab, he responded with one thousand red roses with a precious stone in the center of each rose.

Meant as a romantic gesture, it made Jezebel so mad. "What in the world does any woman do with this many flowers?" she asked her father crossly. He laughed and shook his head. "He is a man in love Jezebel. His thinking is not clear right now." Jezebel had her staff dismantle the roses and remove the precious stones. A jeweler was commissioned to come and create exquisite pieces of jewelry for Jezebel. The rose petals were crushed to make perfume and fragrant lotions and oils. A lot of perfume, lotions, and oil.

King Ethbaal took notice that Ahab did not heed his advice about Jezebel preferring rose bushes instead of cut roses. He wondered what other advice the future son-in-law would disregard that he had given him.

Jezebel accepted many gifts from King Ahab over the course of the next year. She and her father traveled to visit King Ahab's palace one more time during that year to allow the Princess and the King to get to know each other better. It was an uncomfortable time for Jezebel, yet King Ahab was so happy. He spoke endlessly of his childhood and his hopes and dreams. He was an emotional man, getting tears in his eyes as he spoke of his mother and frather and how they died too soon. Jezebel inwardly scoffed at this sign of weakness. Even though he always did his best to try and impress her, Jezebel rarely let him think that she was impressed.

After their travels and Jezebel agreed to marry King Ahab, then she went back home to prepare for the marital arrangement.

The female companions that her Father had commissioned for her were constantly around Jezebel during the day, at the King's request, and they were getting on her nerves. They loved to gossip and tell jokes and laugh and pick on each other. Her father had felt like she needed "girl time" since she didn't have any friends. Jezebel had been a loner most of her life and she did not like the company of other women. They were usually jealous of her and it was just awkward. Many days she would feign a headache just to make them all leave and she could have some peace and quiet.

On one particular day, one of the girls whose name was Donita, who was pretty but exceedingly dumb was running a marathon with her mouth.

Jezebel always believed the girl was just pretending to be that brainless, surely no one was really that stupid! She talked all the time and seemed to have no filter about her mouth. She would say the most vulgar things. Whatever she thought of, came out of her mouth even if it embarrassed other people, she didn't seem to know she was classless.

Her father, an Earl would have been sick if he knew how immoral his daughter was! Donita would brag about watching the servants having sex in the dark corners of the castle, or herself kissing a young servant girl who now believed she was in love with Donita.

Jezebel wished she could have the braggart's tongue cut out just to shut her up.

Every week was a new topic of some daring or dangerous sexual activity Donita was doing or trying but today the girl was beyond limits. Jezebel tried to be a little nice to her and asked her to tone it down a bit. The details of her exploits were raw and disgusting... However, Donita tried to be the center of attention at all times even if it annoyed everyone. It enraged Jezebel and she enjoyed rattling this girl's cage every chance she got. Since Jezebel was the Princess and Donita never would be a Princess, that made Jezebel always got the last word.

On a particular day, Donita had everyone's attention telling them about her latest lover. "He loves to take me in the stable and ride me like the horses do each other! His manhood is big like the horses." she gloated. "Aren't you afraid of getting a baby?" one of the virgins asked timidly. Donita said "Not at all. He says we can't make a baby the way we do it! And so technically I am still a virgin so I can marry as a virgin." The young women all gasp at her vulgarity. Donita threw her long red hair back and laughed loudly! She loved to shock the other girls. "Don't decide until you try it!" she yelled out wickedly.

Jezebel confronted her "Donita are you fooling around with another stable boy?" Donita smiled and said "He is no boy, Princess. He is a monster of a man." Jezebel smiled and shook her head and said "Instead of playing with monsters, why don't we just tell your father you are ready to be married and let him find you a man instead of a monster?"

Donita smiled and answered, "I may not be able to sit down from pain, but I am very impressed with that monster and I am not ready to be some wimpy old man's boring wife."

Since she was all but referring to Jezebel's up-and-coming marriage to the older King Ahab, this incensed Jezebel. The other girls froze amid the showdown between Jezebel and the braggart.

Jezebel then told her that in spite of her happiness she was going to be dismissing her from her service.

" I'm so sorry for you and your monster Donita, but as you know, I am to be married soon, and well, I just don't see a need for you in my new life. You are an insult to women. You may gather your belongings and leave now."

Donita hesitated to see if Jezebel was serious...when realizing she was, she burst into tears, "You can't! I mean I can't, I can't be separated from him yet. Our affair is so fresh. Please! I have never had a man make me feel like he does. Please don't separate us. If you send me home it will have to be over and I need to feel like he makes me, feel before I get married off to some boring old man who has no way of making me feel this way!"

Apparently again Donita forgot she was there for service to the Princess!

Not to mention she just insulted Jezebel again by making a negative reference to her soon to be groom. All of the other girls were frozen where they stood! They could not believe Donita's disrespect and saw her headed for a breakdown! Donita's eyes were like huge pools of unfallen tears and her face was distorted as if ready to explode.

Jezebel stared coolly at Donita and said, "Your happiness is not the least bit of my concern. It never has been. Life is a sacrifice at times Donita. Please try to control yourself."

When she saw that Jezebel was serious about dismissing her, Donita stormed out of the room slamming the door behind her, knocking over and breaking an expensive vase. This was a huge insult to the Princess. Everyone knew you did not leave until given permission, you certainly didn't storm anywhere and now she has destroyed a favorite vase of the Princess!?!

Knowing exactly where Donita went off to; Jezebel sent for her Father and to Donita's Father and told them she was so very worried about Donita disappearing while upset.

"She may be at the stables admiring the horses. She seems to have developed an appetite for them lately. I am just very concerned for her well-being, the way she ran away concerned me greatly. I had just let her know that I was going to have to dismiss her from my service since I was leaving the country and I did not want to take her from her family. I will accompany you to see if I can comfort her" Jezebel said to the men with much concern."

Bringing 2 guards; the King and the Earl, Donita's Father, escorted Jezebel to the stables. As they approached, they could hear Donita's muffled cries and screams; they thought she was in pain and they began to run to her rescue! When they arrived at the area she was in, they saw a large, naked stable hand violently raping Donita. They all saw he was taking her from behind like the horses do. The man's hand was over her mouth and the other hand had hold of her hip.

The guards immediately struck the stable hand in the back of the head with the flat side of his sword, killing him instantly, much to Donita's despair. Donita flung herself on top of the stable hand and screamed "Nooooo!" over his dead body. She looked like a crazy person jumping to her feet and screaming at the guards, not even aware of her nakedness, nor the fact that the King and her own father were present. Donita was screaming "Nooo! You killed him. He wasn't hurting me; he was loving me!" The guards tried to cover her with a horse blanket and she fought them like a tiger. Her father stood there shocked, ashamed and confused.

Jezebel smiled at Donita and turned to her father and said sweetly "We probably should go back to the castle father, this looks like a matter that you nor I should be involved in."

The King quickly grasped her arm turning her away and said "Yes, my dear let's go back inside." and they promptly left.

Donita began to scream at them from behind their back "Jezebel YOU are the reason this has happened. You..." Then there was a sound like a clap and then Donita crumbled to the stable floor. Her own father had knocked her out cold to keep her from disrespecting the Princess publicly.

Donita was never to be seen in court again. Her disgraced father, the Earl was sent to the outermost part of the country taking his family with him.

One evening while returning to the castle from a social outing, a young woman with 3 small children ran in front of the carriage that carried Jezebel. She heard the guards yelling and the children crying so Jezebel looked out to see what was going on. The young mother saw Jezebel peek out and cried out to her, "Oh Princess! Please help me. My husband has abandoned us. He went in search of work, food or help. He has not returned. We have no family here, no food, no money. I do not ask for myself but for my children, please I beg of you, can you give me food to feed my babies?"

The young mother's eyes rolled back and she collapsed in front of the carriage, maybe from fear and hunger but from the look on her face she was more than likely dead. Jezebel yelled for her guards to move her out of the way so they could pass.

"The children?" a younger guard inquired.

"Throw them to the sacrifice fire to Ba'al. At least they will serve a purpose." Jezebel said with a laugh. The guard looked puzzled, as if unsure of what to do. Jezebel narrowed her eyes and spoke through gritted teeth "Do you have sons, guard?" he said "Yes. I have 2."

"Question my word again and you and your sons will be sacrificed like these 3 brats are." He bowed to her and turned away to gather the small children. Jezebel put her hand to her head as they proceeded down the road. She thought to herself, "Why do people have to irritate me so? There is so much to do before I move to my new kingdom. I hate these little minor distractions."

When she arrived back at the castle she was told there was a visitor from her new country that request to see her.

"His business?" Jezebel asked the manservant. She assumed it was a messenger with even more gifts from King Ahab.

"He said his name is Sir Nivek and he was sent from the new kingdom to prepare her highness for the transition."

Jezebel left him waiting and went to clean up from her brief visit outside the castle; but it was worth the wait the gentleman had. She was stunning as she arrived at her father's office. "Your new dress is beautiful my daughter!" the King gushed. She smiled and thanked him. They talked for a few minutes before sending for the visitor.

Jezebel and her father were waiting for him to be brought to them in her father's office and for a second Jezebel felt anxious in her stomach. Maybe it was the fact she was really advancing into her new life...As he entered the room, a gasp almost escaped from Jezebel's mouth. There was an immediate electric shock that hit her cold heart as she looked into the eyes of this man.

He was tall and had long black curls for hair and piercing grey eyes! He was a beautiful man. His smile caressed her heart and his eyes danced when he looked at her. He was smiling at her with his eyes!

He was being professional and respectful yet her heart took it as playful. She watched his beautiful mouth saying words that she could not hear because she was so distracted by the movement of his perfect lips. This was the first time Jezebel had ever FELT anything like this. When he bent to kiss her hand, they both were astonished to see she was trembling.

She was unable to look away from him, suddenly afraid he was not real.

"Jezebel, are you okay daughter?" her father asked perplexed by her silence.

She blushed deeply, probably for the first time in years then she did something she had never done before...she stuttered... "I, I, I am fine. Father."

The visitor looked to her father the King and inquired of his health, in attempt to divert the attention from the Princess. His first act of heroism, rescuing a floundering Princess!

He and the King made small talk for a few minutes. "My King sends you his deepest regards Sire. He inquires of your well-being and sends his respect and admiration."

Jezebel calmed herself and then spoke up. "Sir, I shall require a series of meetings with you to organize the, ah, the details of the transition to the new Kingdom."

He smiled and said, "I am at your complete disposal, my Queen". At that moment Jezebel's heart began to beat so fast she could taste her heartbeat. Her Father arose from his chair and lazily said "I will leave you two to the task. I need a rest." and hobbled out of the door. Jezebel looked at the man and said "I suppose you had better start at the beginning." he smiled and nodded to her.

They sat down in the chairs by the window and he brought out some paperwork filled with details about the kingdom. "What is your name and position again?" He smiled because he knew she had not been listening to him when he first entered.

"I am Nivek, head counsel to the King. I have been in King Ahab's service for over 20 years."

She studied his face, the slight touch of gray at his temple, a few slight wrinkles near his perfect brown eyes, and the way his eyes seemed to dance, this man could truly smile with his eyes! Although she had many questions, they talked for hours, not about the kingdom business but about politics, food, their hobbies, their upbringing, everything but business. It seemed like a conversation between old friends.

Jezebel knew without a doubt she had never been in love before until this day. He was smart, he was strong, handsome, brave, witty, charming, intelligent, kind, well-mannered, level headed. Everything she ever wanted in a man but had never found or even knew she wanted!

For hours she laughed and enjoyed herself so much. It wasn't until the servants came to call her for dinner that she realized how long they had been together. The servants noticed she was not escorted by her father, nor chaperoned with this visitor, and also hadn't dressed for dinner, but they didn't dare say anything. The servants were astonished by the thing on the face of the princess...a smile, a real, genuine smile.

They had not ever really seen a real smile of happiness on her face. She was normally all about business and busy being cruel. The servers noticed she looked younger, relaxed, even happy.

The gentleman sat where she motioned him to; next to her, breaking all protocol of the royal household. The King moved down to be closer to them which sent everyone scrambling to move dishes and chairs.

The dinner conversation was about fishing and hunting. The topics Jezebel never discussed! Even the King was in a jovial mood during dinner. He loved to see his daughter laughing and enjoying herself.

The next few days were consumed with meetings between Jezebel and

Nivek. He was finally able to convince her to listen to his information about the coming nuptials and her new home. He explained how many servants they employed and was impressed to know she wanted to know about every detail that surrounded the king's duties, servants, friends and his properties.

She knew the king was one that sort of believed in the God of Abraham and she had every intention of changing all of that when she came into her Kingdom but she felt the need not to share this with Nivek. She did not want to do anything to change her in his sight. He believed she was beautiful and kind and smart, she thought to herself. "I want this man for my own, even though I don't know how to arrange it, I am in love and seeing things so differently now. The world is worth living in just so I can see him one more time"

Everyday their feelings grew more powerful of each other. The were free to roam the hillside on horseback, or go into any room of the Castle unescorted. The King quietly issued a proclamation that he trusted his daughter and her judgment above anyone else, and anyone who opposed her, opposed him. Maybe in his wicked heart, he was giving his permission for her to experience something he knew she would never have with the wimpy king he was marrying her off too.

The King temporarily gave a vacation to all the court including the companions; freeing up Jezebels time to do as she pleased. At least he could give his daughter this time with a man that she seemed to admire. Just a few servants were left to run the house.

So while Jezebel and Nivek picnicked in the country, danced in the Kings court, ate every meal together, played like school kids, ran like teenagers at times, had discussions about everything under the sun, they still did not cross any legal sexual lines. Nivek did not physically cheat on his wife and Jezebel was still a virgin. They were like best friends who could tell each other everything and know it would always be kept secret. They never challenged each other or argued.

Nivek poured out his heart to Jezebel and explained that his life with his wife was just for the children. They didn't really have a life together. He worked and went home, spent time with the children, met their needs. And even though he never condemned his wife or spoke ill of her, he never praised her except to say she is a good mother.

Jezebel usually changed the subject quickly because she didn't want to even think of sharing Nivek with anyone at this point. They were learning all about each other and life was so free and fun.

It was so wonderful like they were living in a dream world! Sadly, we all know that eventually we all wake up from dreams.

It was night and the princess was alone in her room and she realized she was crying on her pillow. "I do not cry!" she yelled out, then she buried her face in the pillow and cried more. "He is only on the next floor from me. I can smell him on my hands, feel his lips on my fingers. Why have I never known this feeling before? If there is one god, he is cruel to let me feel this way about a man only to know I can never spend my life with him?" She stopped crying and sat up in the bed and whispered "I can force him to leave his wife and come to me. We can be together!" then she felt sick to her stomach and collapsed back on the bed "He would never allow that to happen. He is a good man, loyal and faithful to his family and his King. He would probably move away and

I would never see him again. Oh! I couldn't bare that!" she fell back on the pillows with a sigh. She curled up and wondered "Am I mad like my mother? Does her illness plaque me? Why do I let these feelings consume me like a fire?" She got out of bed and found her journal and wrote these words by candlelight...

"I am under the influence of this spectacular temptation, which I have resisted not and in which he has over mastered me without me drawing a breath of opposition. He could lure me to any life, to any death, he could draw me to anything of which I hate, He could demand that I run away far away with him and I would leave right now wearing only my nightclothes and a robe! 'Your wishes, my command.'. If only you would give the word, you could have me with such ridiculous ease. Hopelessly yours my love"

She sighed, then closed the book that held her most private thoughts and held it to her chest. Tears flowed again as she went back to her bed and hoped to dream of him.

Nivek was her guest for nearly one month. It was undoubtedly the happiest time of her entire life. He asked her once how she had managed all this time to sidestep love and she did not have an answer for him.

With huge love-filled eyes, she whispered, "My own belief is that love found me, I did not go in search of it."

He smiled but she saw torment in his eyes. He knew he would never have her because he belonged to another but his heart was burning for this woman who had never known love until he walked into her heart.

Later as he sat in his room, guilt and confusion swept over Nivek. He knew he was feeling love for Jezebel. How could he have let this happen?

He did not love her like he loved his wife. It was a different feeling. He loved Jezebel's free spirit and her laughter. He loved her eyes that looked at him like he was the most amazing man in the world. She was not mean, nor did she nag or berate him. She didn't point out his faults or flaws. She made him smile even when she wasn't in the room. He could tell she wanted him body and soul.

His wife had quit allowing him to share her bed 4 years ago. Every once in a great while when she wanted something, she would allow him to come to her room, but not often. She didn't enjoy kissing and cuddling and holding each other before and after. She had always just wanted him to perform the sex act and get out. The quicker the better. She did not like to have her hair messed up.

Nivek loved that his wife was a good mother and she was kind to everyone else in the world. She never disgraced him at his King's court and always acted like a lady. But she had an upbringing that molded her mind to believe that men were dishonorable, disgusting creatures, not to be trusted and to be used to gather great gains. She was one to put great faith in fortune. She wanted Nivek to work as much as he could to keep them secure, yet she did little to encourage him with something to come home to. All he did seemed to never be enough. She wanted a bigger house, bigger carriages, and more servants, he gave her everything and more yet nothing ever pleased her, nonetheless he never once stopped trying. He loved his children. Of all of his accomplishments, they were the best things he had ever done in his life.

He was an honorable, trustworthy man. That is exactly why the king had sent him here to educate Jezebel. He knew if the King had even dreamed he had these feelings for his bride-to-be, he would be executed publicly. His own family would be executed before his eyes, then He would be executed. This had to end. He knew that it was time to leave. It was time to go back home and pick up where he left off with his family and his King.

Nivek had received a message from the King inquiring as to the visit and begging him to give Jezebel his admiration and to tell her that he could hardly wait for his life to begin with her. Nivek took that as a final indication he must go quickly before this emotional affair went too far to come back from.

Jezebel was up early, eager to attend to her duties so she could visit with him. She was anxious for some reason she could not explain. The staff prepared a beautiful breakfast and they were served in the garden at Jezebel's request. After a wonderful meal, the king excused himself and the two were left alone. Nivek cleared his throat and spoke softly to Jezebel,

"My queen, the time has come that I must take my leave, tomorrow. I am expected back at the castle as we have diplomats arriving in a week's time for a conference. I have much to prepare for" He immediately saw the injury in her eyes and wanted to go to her and console her. Her eyes locked with his... they said so much without saying anything.

"It will not be long before you are to arrive at the castle. I believe there are 83 more days before the wedding party is to arrive," he said lightly.

She asked hopefully, "Will you come back?"

He stood up and faced away from her. "No, the King has sent word for me that he is requiring my assistance but please know time will go by quickly. You have much preparation to attend before your wedding day."

Jezebel felt her eyes stinging with tears, she felt like she might faint if she were not sitting down. The moment he dreaded the most was here. He was having to let go of her and it was ripping his heart out. He slowly turned to look at her. Fear was in her eyes. Not fear of him, but fear of losing him. Nivek tried to be brave for both of them and smiled at her as he said

"This time with you has been so incredible. I have gotten to know what an amazing woman you are." then his gaze fell to the ground as he said, " The king is the luckiest man in the entire world!" Nivek said those words with a sad smile. Jezebel was trying to find her words, "I ...am neither incredible nor amazing. I am almost panic-stricken at the prospect of your leaving." she looked down at her half-empty plate. "In all my life I have never felt this way about another living person."

He came to sit next to her and took her hand. "Love is a very strange emotion. It captures the hearts of unsuspecting victims and then circumstances force their way in and cause larger more dangerous disruptions. They are like small demons that run amuck seducing hearts and then destroying them as quickly. If I had met you first, if I had known you first, I would have done everything in my power to be yours. But as you already know, the truth is I have a wife, that I love and 5 children. All girls. They need me and I need them. They are my source of continued existence and strength. You, however, will be my source of will and determination. You will always be the Queen of my heart." Her tears spilled as did his.

"I don't want to lose you," she said pitifully.

"You could no more lose me, than you could lose the Moon and Stars. It is not in your ability. Even when I am not here with you, I will be here with you" he said kissing her palms and drawing her hands to her heart. Her tears began to flow so beautifully. Nivek was overwhelmed. He could not remember the last time a beautiful woman cried for him, for his love, desiring him as she did. It was both a beautiful and cruel sight for both of them.

He stared into her eyes and whispered, "I have a request of you Jezebel" "Anything my love"

He asked her to have her servants draw her a hot bath for that evening then send them away. "Send them far away demanding that you wish not to be disturbed!" She nodded yes, he squeezed her hands and walked out of the garden. Jezebel was confused but did as he asked her to.

That evening as the servants left her alone for her bath, her heart was racing.

Did Nivek just want her to relax in the hot bath? He never said. Maybe he thought she just needed time to be without stress. Perhaps he might join her?

Jezebel was soaking in the hot bath water as she heard him enter the room and she looked up into his eyes. He leaned down and kissed her hands, then he kissed her forehead, and her eyes and her nose and her cheeks. Her heart was surely going to burst open from excitement and happiness. He took the sponge and began to bathe her. For a moment she was embarrassed, as no man had ever seen her naked, but embarrassment evolved into intimacy as she looked at this man in his eyes and saw the love and devotion that he felt for her. He stepped behind her and washed her hair. His fingers on her scalp were like nothing she had ever felt. Then he moved to her body. Every inch of her body was ingested into his mind as he washed her fingers and arms, her neck, and shoulders, He helped her to her feet and washed each breast, her stomach, her most intimate parts, her legs, her feet, and then her toes. Jezebel was trembling not from being cold, but from passion and desire. He took the pitcher and poured clean water over her gently, rinsing the soap from her completely and drying her off limb by limb.

From her most intimate parts to her fingers and toes. It was truly the most treasured moment she had ever shared with another human being.

He did not molest her, he did not have intercourse with her, he cleansed her body and encompassed her soul. He studied her body as to take in every curve, every inch of her to burn into his mind.

Nivek then took oil and rubbed it between his hands and rubbed her body completely. Neither spoke, they just shared in this sensual, loving act.

After he finished putting the oil on her, he stood in front of her looking at her young, perfect body. He smiled, and then he poured the white nightgown over her head and onto her body. Tears were spilling from his eyes as he whispered

"I have never seen one so beautiful in all of my life." He turned her away from him and dried her hair some more. He stood behind her and held her for some time. Then he let her go and walked out of the room. Jezebel wondered for a minute if she dreamed the entire thing because she was in such a daze. She felt drunk with wine, though she had not had one sip. She went to her bed and waited to see if he would come make love to her, to devour her, to have his way with her.

He did not come to her.

She must have drifted off to sleep waiting for him because she woke up and began to cry as soon as she realized she heard horses and carriages leaving the castle. Knowing that her heart had just left her behind, Jezebel called for her servants and asked them to call for the doctor.

She was weak and trembling. "I feel ill. Please get the doctor, do not disturb my father." The doctor who lived there at the castle came running in quickly. The King was notified against her will. She told him that she was sick and needed something to make her not feel so sick to her stomach and something to help her rest.

She lied and told him she had not been sleeping. The doctor gave her medication that allowed Jezebel to sleep for about 3 days. She wanted to be away from the world to heal from her heartache. She knew she didn't want to die even if she felt like she was dying inside. The prospect of seeing him again gave her the will to live.

Later, her young servant Amanda said "Princess you must have had a fever, you kept calling for a certain guest, then you would collapse again when you realized it was me and not him sitting here." Jezebel straightened up and said "Do not mistake my illness for weakness and do not repeat what you have heard me say thru fever. If you do, I swear will have my father, The King, shall behead you and all of your family. Do you understand?" the young girl nearly fainted as she whispered, "Yes of course. I am sorry."

The young girl did know one thing, she knew she must warn the staff that the old Jezebel was back amongst them.

By the next day Amanda the servant had been sent away and a new servant was to attend to the Princess Jezebel. The servant girl hadn't done anything wrong; Jezebel just couldn't stand someone reminding her of her actions under medication, especially someone who witnessed her scream Nivek's name during her illness. Once Jezebel could gather her thoughts, she realized Nivek did the only thing he could do to protect them both from vicious gossip that might get back to the King. He left so there would be no emotional scene or situations to report back. She wondered if any gossip had already been reported since his stay was so long. But surely, he would have warned her had he heard any such rumors.

Jezebel kept looking at her hands, the hands he kissed, and held.

It took her a few days to get back on the right track mentally. Her world had been turned upside down from the moment they announced he had arrived. She was determined to get on with her new kingdom, and keep him as close to her as she could.

The next weeks Jezebel worked fervently to pack all of her personal belongings, get fitted for her wedding gown, hired more staff to attend to her father and trained them as she wanted them. Her father announced that there would be 3 large dinner parties in celebration of her wedding. Jezebel had hoped Nivek would come again but her father told her that not even King Ahab was coming. These parties were in her appreciation and he was not inviting King Ahab.

"These parties are for honoring the bride my dear, you will be lavished with presents!" her father laughed. This did not comfort Jezebel. No present could touch her heart except for the "presence" of Nivek.

The parties were extravagant but none too impressive for Jezebel. She smiled and was an adequate hostess but always felt anxious as if time couldn't pass quickly enough.

Her appetite was not what it once was and she was looking leaner than usual. Her Father showed up in the garden one evening while she was there alone. "My dearest, are you concerned about your new position in life?" her father asked with great concern. "You have been so distant from me since your illness." Jezebel managed a smile and said "No Father, I am okay. Just thinking. Maybe I am just a little tired from all the parties we have had lately." she said in an upbeat voice. "Well you haven't been eating much, you have lost some weight and I am just concerned about you my dearest." her father hesitated, not wanting to make her angry. Too late, Jezebel snapped at him, "So I look gaunt and sickly is that what you are implying Father? Did you ever think maybe I am a little nervous about going to another country?" The king smiled and said "Absolutely not my daughter. Fear is not an emotion you possess."

Jezebel smiled back at him and said "You are right Father. I am not afraid. Excited, anxious, willing but not afraid. I don't even know why I said that." She laughed then sighed and sat back down. "I will miss you Father and I hope that you come and see me often," Jezebel said softly. "Oh, now you know I will my precious. I must know they are treating you with the respect and love you deserve." the King answered quickly.

"Ahab has been decorating a section of the castle just for when you come and visit Father. There will be rooms for you and any guest you bring. He wants you to feel at home too." Jezebel said smiling. At that moment a servant came to the garden entrance and announced that there was a guest waiting for the Princess. Jezebel nearly ran out of the garden, if the King had not touched her arm to stop her, she would have.

"It may not be him dear. Calm yourself." Jezebel stopped and took a breath and headed inside the castle with her father in tow.

As they approached the foyer area Jezebel noticed about 6 women. There were no men there. They bowed as she entered the area. The first one spoke with enthusiasm "I am Joan. King Ahab has hired me to assist you with any wedding details. These are my assistants." The others stayed bowed until Jezebel mumbled "Arise." Joan had swatches of fabric and lace, examples of flowers and colors, tulle, ribbon, beads, pearls, and every imaginable idea for the wedding and reception. Jezebel became extremely aggravated and snapped at her "Don't you think it is a little late to be doing all of this? We should have started months ago!" Joan looked perplexed and said "Princess, I beg your most humble apology, however, I have requested 5 times in the last 2 months to come and you have not responded to me. I even had the messenger ask you to sign the notices to prove you were receiving them. King Ahab finally just insisted that I come now, while there is still time to give you the wedding of your dreams."

Jezebel felt her face flush, but she turned away from the woman to hide it then said, "I have had many things to get in order here before leaving my Father."

Joan was very calm and pleasant saying, "Of course you have! I completely understand." Since you have traveled so far Joan, let you and your staff rest this evening after dinner and we will begin our planning, first thing after breakfast tomorrow." Jezebel suggested. Joan smiled with relief and agreed.

Jezebel tried to eat a little more at dinner since she knew her father was watching. She also indulged in a cake dessert with rich, sweet whipped cream poured over the top. This made her father laugh because he knew she was doing it just to please him. She smiled a big smile at him. Suddenly the King's heart hurt a little. He would miss her so much. She had been the brightest light in his entire world. The King looked apround the room and wondered how this place would feel without her presence and it made him sad. He called over his servant Jovan and told him to play music and let the women dance! This was not a usual event in this castle so the people were surprised and happy to do so.

Jezebel did not dance but she didn't complain about the dancing either. She could tell her father was feeling emotional and she wanted him to be happy.

For several hours the party raged on. It was a nice little, impromptu party for the visitors and the staff. The people drank wine and whiskey and enjoyed themselves. Her father clapped his hands to the music and even got a few individual dances from the younger ladies present. He didn't have to dance. They would dance for him. He loved that.

Jezebel called for her father's favorite massage artist and an additional woman to be sent to his room when he was ready to retire. Her father was getting older but he still had a strong desire for good food and bad women.

The next morning the servants escorted everyone to the conference room with 3 large tables, and the wedding planning day was in full motion.

Joan had asked Jezebel to bring any ideas that she had with her to the meeting. Jezebel was embarrassed to show up empty-headed and empty-handed.

"I thought the King would handle all of the details," she said warily. Joan smiled and said "No, most women want to plan their wedding. There are some traditions that some women won't get married without performing." She wasn't rude or snappish so Jezebel couldn't be mad at her but she irritated her at any rate. "How many guests are we expecting?" Jezebel asked. "More than 3000 people will be in attendance at the reception and more than 2000 for the wedding ceremony," Glenda said easily. "You don't think those numbers are more than a little outrageous?" Jezebel balked. Joan's eyes opened wide and she said "These numbers are made known to me by Sir Nivek himself. The King's right-hand man." Jezebel felt faint at his very name. She had to go and sit down and compose herself.

Joan cleared her throat and said "I am sure that this can be overwhelming Princess. The King insists that cake and punch be served to all who attend the reception. It is a royal celebration that includes the masses. The people are kind and decent folk, they will not abuse the King's generosity. He wants them to share in his happiness. It is not every day our King gets married. This is his first marriage and the people are so happy to welcome you as their Queen! As for the number at the ceremony, there are foreign dignitaries, relatives, business associates, religious leaders, community leaders, and close personal friends of the King's that will be in attendance. Those details have already been decided. I just wanted to share the details with you, for your knowledge and to see if you had any last-minute changes you wished for."

Jezebel thought about demanding that anyone who was not personally invited (meaning the masses of the country) bring their own homemade cake and punch to celebrate. But she did not want to anger the King who had already decreed such a holiday event.

She thought to herself, "Wastefulness such as this could break a kingdom. This nitwit of a king is just giving away a fortune in cake and punch alone.

He should be very happy I am coming to rescue his kingdom from him"

The next few days were spent ironing out the details. Where would her father sit? What color horses did she want to bring her to the castle? What color punch did she want to be served? Which flowers did she want in her wedding bouquet? Jezebel suddenly felt very tired and excused herself leaving poor Joan with even more unanswered questions.

Jezebel went to her room and cried. Here she was planning a royal wedding with a man she didn't even know; all the while loving, adoring, and longing for another man she could not have.

She got up from the bed and grabbed the bucket by the door and emptied her stomach like she had almost every night for nearly 2 months. Her nerves were so bad she shook. Jezebel took out her journal and held it against her body in the bed. Night after night she had read all the entries of Nivek and their wonderful time together. She had marked all the witty comments and compliments he had given her. She even had flowers pressed between two sheets that he had given her. Jezebel had noted every item they shared at every meal. The book was a constant reminder of the best time in her entire life. The book held her will to live and her key to death. If it were ever discovered by anyone, she would be killed for betraying her betrothed, as would Nivek. She wrote to him night after night in that book pouring out her deepest desires and begging him to come to her.

Jezebel did not know what to do with the book. She couldn't destroy it; it was her life line to Nivek. However, if she didn't destroy it, it could mean her death and his.

A small knock came at the door. It was her father. "Jezebel. I need to talk to you," he called through the door. She opened it. Her father looked upset. "Father, what is wrong?" He walked in and took her hands and they sat on the end of her bed. "Jezebel, King Ahab has requested that your mother accompany us to your wedding." Jezebel let out a little laugh and said "You know father we never did explain to him that she is incapacitated." He smiled and said "As embarrassing as this is, maybe I should just take someone in her place to pretend she is your mother. It would save us both a lot of discomfort." "Or we could just say she recently died, father. I could say it is too painful to talk about and he would not dare approach the subject again. You can have an escort and no one would dare say anything." The king looked relieved and said "Yes that is even better. You know their customs are slightly different from ours my dear. I just didn't want to insult your husband." Jezebel hugged her father but rolled her eyes behind his back. Just to hear the word husband, annoyed her.

By day five, all arrangements had been finalized and Joan and her staff were back en route to prepare for the wedding. Jezebel never once inquired about Sir Nivek in case there had been any gossip, but the entire visit she was desperate to ask.

She so wanted to go back with Joan as a stowaway in her carriage so she could see Nivek. A small smile crossed Jezebel's face at the wicked thought.

There were less than 2 weeks until Jezebel and her father were going to make the trip to her new country. Jezebel tried to eat as much as she could to replace her weight and took in multiple spa treatments to make her feel even more beautiful.

However, her nerves never seemed to steady themselves.

Her father had commissioned a magnificent large, comfortable carriage for their extensive trip.

The etiquette was that Jezebel and her father and her staff would stay at a nearby Castle belonging to Earl Easel for the 3 days prior to the wedding. The name of the Castle was Morriswood. It was amazingly beautiful with marble and stone floors and fabulous gardens. A beautiful water fountain was in the foyer and there was a welcome sign arranged for Jezebel and her party. The walkway was lit by luminaries at night...It was stunning. It even impressed Jezebel. Earl Easel's wife, Zeldamar, was a perfect hostess. She was a perfectionist who handled every detail right down to the candy on the guest bed pillows.

On the second day, the seamstress came to visit with Jezebel.

Her wedding gown was in a room all on its own and it looked so gorgeous standing on its own in the room.

It had been attached to a body form that held the dress up as if an invisible body were wearing it. It was spectacular, it was stunning, it was lavish, it was...too big.

Jezebel had lost at least 12 lbs. in the last 3 months. She had grieved so much. The seamstress told her not to fret, that she had always known how to fix the tiniest of details. "This I can fix, now if you had grown

6 inches taller, then we would have had a problem!" the seamstress teased trying to make Jezebel more at ease. Jezebel smiled a little. The remeasuring was done and the miracle work began immediately. By evening the dress would be ready to be tried on again. This time it would fit flawlessly. Jezebel was so happy, just as a bride-to-be should be. However, she was pleased the dress would fit so that when she saw Nivek she wouldn't look ridiculous or unfit. She would look amazing.

She practically floated outside to the garden to relax, then headed back to her room for she was nearly ready for her massage. Tomorrow would be the day she saw him again at last! She happily walked back into her room and immediately upon entering, noticed her journal was lying on the bed.

There was a sound that came from Jezebel's mouth like nothing she had ever heard from herself. It was a cross between a cry and a groan. She grabbed her journal and flew down the stairs screaming for Earl Easles wife.

The entire household came running. "Who was in my room?" she demanded angrily, screaming again "Who?" a pudgy servant girl raised her hand.

"I knocked before I went in. I was told to change your sheets, make the bed and tidy your room your highness." Jezebel slapped her hard, and the young servant girls face was red on both cheeks.

Jezebel then hit her across the head, hard with her journal.

"You are a sneaky underhanded wench. You went thru my things and now I have expensive jewelry that is missing! You thief, you dishonest pig of a person!" Jezebel exploded on the girl.

The servant was trying to interject and explain but the strike on the head with the heavy journal left her stunned. The Earl's wife was embarrassed and jumped in to grab hold of the girl. She demanded that her male servant take the girl out immediately and have her horsewhipped until she told where the stolen jewelry was.

"Where is my dead Mother's jewelry?" Jezebel screamed after her.

The servant girl had no idea what Jezebel was talking about because there had been no jewelry. The truth is, Jezebel was trying to soil the girl's reputation in case she had read the journal.

The girl never even opened the book she found under the pillow. She just left it on the bed so the Princess would find it since the bed was made.

"You must send her away. I cannot stay in this house with the likes of her. Do you understand me?" Jezebel said nervously. The Earl's wife said "yes of course" and kept apologizing. She was embarrassed down to her shoes. It had been such an honor for the Princess to come here ahead of the Royal Wedding. Jezebel was so upset she could not hear what the Earl's wife was saying, she just walked back upstairs and collapsed against her bedroom door holding her journal. The ending could have been so much worse. She could hear horrific screams coming from the servant girl who was being whipped, but Jezebel just thought "Hmp serves her right for coming in my room."

That evening the Earl's wife was relieved to see Jezebel and her party come down for dinner. They all acted as if nothing had happened which made her feel even better. Her chefs and bakers had worked furiously to put out incredible spreads. She couldn't help but be proud how everything was going so smoothly, but still she felt terrible about what happened earlier. She walked outside to join the Princess to look at the night sky. "Your Highness, please allow me to apologize again for today. I have several pieces of jewelry I would be honored for you to have in place of your dear Mother's jewelry that is missing."

Jezebel looked at her, smiled and said sweetly, "Oh never mind about that. I found those pieces behind my jewelry box. I just thought they were missing. They must have fallen behind it. But thank you for your offer. I think I will retire now, tomorrow's the big day!"

The Earl's wife was stunned! Her male servant had nearly beaten a devoted servant girl to death today with a horse whip for stealing jewelry that was never stolen. The girl was hideously beaten and sent away from the only home she had ever known. The Earl's wife felt nauseated. The worst part was that the soon-to-be Queen wasn't even remorseful, not at all!

"What kind of monster is the King getting for a wife?" The Earl's wife wondered to herself as she wiped away the tears of regret from her eyes.

"I must find a way to make a way to make it up to that poor servant girl." She thought for a moment of the terror in the young girl's eyes as she was being yanked away for her torture, and she bit her lip to keep from crying out. Her eyes looked to Heaven and she said "God please forgive me!"

Jezebel slept fitfully because of anxiety. She wanted the morning to hurry and get there so she could see her love.

She was up and dressed and ready way before the staff arrived to dress her for her wedding. She watched from the window as her father and all the others left for their 3-mile journey to the Castle.

Her carriage was pulled by 8 solid white horses and was the last to leave Morriswood. It was incredible to look at. The horses were huge and the carriage specially made so that the Queen to be could be seen by all and armed guards followed behind her clear carriage. Jezebel felt like she was in a bubble. It irritated her how slow time was dragging by. The carriage was being pulled at a respectable slow pace so the masses could greet the Queen to-be.

She reflected on her life and realized this was probably the purpose of her life. To lead others but not to be led. These horses would lead her to her destiny but she would lead this country. She knew in her heart that she and Nivek would together make this a famous country. People would hear about her for years to come.

Although Nivek could never be king, she was determined to make him the highest-appointed man in the history of appointments. He would be by her side to lead the people. This made her smile so big!

The crowds roared when they saw her smile! Their Queen was happy, smiling at them. What a gift!

She could see the people lined on both sides of the road, throwing flowers and waving and shouting blessings her way but she did not wave back. She smiled, thinking that her time to see her love was so near. The people said it was the most beautiful smile they had ever seen, even though it was curious that she did not wave back. She smiled like an angel, like a woman in love and they were so happy for their King to have found a woman who genuinely loved him!

Her father was waiting to escort her to her husband. The large ceremony made her feel uncomfortable but that was the tradition here so she endured. King Ahab wept openly at the very sight of her. She pressed her lips together to keep from chastising him in front of what appeared to be the entire world. He could not quit crying. She squeezed his hand a little too hard trying to send him a message to tone it down a bit. He smiled as if he understood but the tears kept coming. The high priest that performed the ceremony made several references to God, "before God I pronounce you man and wife, live your lives for God, God is our healer and our hope." Jezebel would have been angry if she knew how much of her wedding ceremony included reference to a God she didn't believe in. But she was too busy looking for Nivek to concentrate too much on what was being said. She finally saw him. He looked like a man that had eaten too much food and drank too much wine. His eyes were huge and he looked like he was about to be sick. Jezebel flashed him a smile and the way he seemed to melt at the sight of her showed her he still needed her. It must have sickened him to see her marry another, just as it sickened her to do so.

Next to him stood a woman that Jezebel assumed was his wife. After what seemed like forever Jezebel was finally able to sit down. She was exhausted. The ceremony had taken hours, now the reception would take more hours.

Jezebel's eyes followed Nivek all around the room and her heart thought it would burst open with happiness. She was so happy to see him again. He tried to steal glances at her and send smiles her way without alerting the King or anyone else for that matter. Long lines of people came to congratulate the royal couple. Everyone could see how radiant the new Queen was and the happiness was nearly contagious. King Ahab was ecstatic. He knew he had made the right choice for a bride. He could tell how happy she was. There were times he thought she would leap out of her chair she was so excited.

Finally, the time she had waited for arrived! Nivek and his wife moved forward to greet the King and Queen and express their deepest, warmest wishes to the new couple. Jezebel could see him whispering in his wife's ear, while he guided her by the elbow. He could not look Queen Jezebel directly in her eyes for fear of giving his feelings away.

Jezebel noticed his wife kept touching her hand to her own stomach. "Are you unwell?" Jezebel asked hopefully.

The King spoke up before Nivek's wife could and said "Queen Jezebel, congratulate Nivek here. He is going to be a father again! What will this be, number 6? All girls so far! I will cross my fingers for you a son this time!"

Nivek smiled weakly at the King and said "Yes my King." He dared not meet Jezebel's cold stare. Jezebel was stunned. He had sex with his wife?

She noticed the wife was not that pretty and didn't look pregnant at all. "How far along are you?" the Queen asked bluntly. The woman blushed and said "Just a few months along. You kept him away from me just long enough for him to miss me! He came back and was so glad to see me!" Nivek looked horrified and said "We must take our leave now." and hurried the woman away from the King and Queen.

Jezebel looked at the King and he shrugged and said "She never has been a favorite of mine. But he is my right arm. I am sure you know by now he is as loyal as they come, so do ignore her. She thinks higher of herself than she is. He doesn't bring her around much anyhow my dear."

People did notice the new Queen did not smile the rest of the day or night. "She looks bored." "Perhaps she is just tired" "She looks overwhelmed!" "Maybe she is" "It's not every day a girl has a wedding this big."

The King and Queen retired later into the evening. Her female servants had helped her bathe and prepare for her wedding night. She smelled like gardenias. King came in and offered her a glass of wine. She shook her head no and he put down his glass and kissed her. His lips were dry and he was nervous but he was smiling. "I am so happy my dearest. You have made me the happiest man alive. I have waited my whole life for you. Other Kings marry for prosperity, fame, fortune, but I have chosen to marry for my heart". She smiled at him. They stood there holding each other. Jezebel could feel his tears falling on her nightgown, but she felt nothing inside. See her heart had failed her earlier in the day when she realized Nivek had left her and went home to his wife and bedded her.

The King and Queen had sex on their wedding night. It was remarkable for him as he screamed out her name in ecstasy. It was exactly as the older women had told her it would be like for her, it hurt briefly, it was messy and then it was over. The King took her two more times before morning, always adoring her and thanking her for becoming his wife. She felt absolutely no emotions and was relieved when the knock came at the door.

The servants came in and escorted the King to his room where he could prepare for the day, and The Queen was helped to clean up and dress in that room. Jezebel asked her servants if the King had his room or if would he share hers. She was told he had his own room and that the current room was hers. This information made her feel a little better. At least she didn't have to worry about him rolling over every night and morning to grope her.

They joined for breakfast and were met with cheers. The news had traveled throughout the castle that the new Queen was a virgin.

The actual proof was on the blood-stained sheet hanging from the Castle walls. Jezebel was mortified! "How dare they know something so personal" she fumed! The King laughed at her and said "Sweetheart, we belong to the people. We are their leaders and they are our family. There was some concern about me taking a bride from another country because they did not know you or your family. But now they have their proof that you were pure they will follow you anywhere." Jezebel stood up and whispered in Ahab's ear. "Sweetheart, I don't need their approval for them to follow me anywhere. Now why don't you follow me back to bed." she walked away from the breakfast table and the King hungrily followed right behind her bringing a plate of biscuits with him.

For a week, days and nights were filled with passion for the King. She rubbed his feet with oils, had artists come and sing songs to him, had female dancers come in to excite him with their dancing and then she would have sex with him all over again. Some nights she would encourage the female dancers to nearly entice him. This excited him, and she would again have sex with him. When he was drained, she would hold him and whisper her desires in his ear. He was completely under her spell, denying her nothing she asked for. She would walk up behind him and press her breast against his back and his knees would nearly buckle. Jezebel would gain her power one calculated move at a time.

Jezebel was taking a tour around the castle when she went into the room that belonged to Nivek. She instantly smelled him in that room. She walked around and felt the shirts that were hanging on hooks. A smile came across her face. It was purely her fantasies of this man that permitted her to put up with her lightning-fast, orgasmic-driven husband. She was shocked when she saw Nivek come thru the door.

Without speaking, they rushed to each other, smothering each other's faces with kisses. "I have missed you so much Jezebel." he moaned between kisses. He backed up, taking her with him to close the door with his body so they would not be discovered. She latched onto him and tore at his shirt and pants. They made love behind an unlocked and unbolted door. Anyone could have walked in and caught them but they were beyond comprehending anything but each other. Fortunately, they were not discovered. However, unfortunately, his love-making skills were so good that Jezebel climaxed for the first time in her life and now honestly believed he was the only man in the world for her. He had to cover her face to keep her screams of ecstasy from being heard all over the castle. She could barely breathe! Her heart was pounding so hard in her chest that she thought it would explode. Nivek held her tightly until her body calmed and he covered her face and neck in kisses.

After several hours of being together, it was Nivek who pulled away and said "We better depart and make our presence known. Surely, they will be missing us by now." Jezebel was almost in an altered state. She was so happy and content that for a moment it frightened her. The girl who wasn't scare of anything felt frightened.

She hesitated as she had something to say, "I love you." she whispered to him. He kissed her long and deep and said "I love you too. Now escape to your room and clean my scent off of you!" she laughed out loud and said "I wish I could smell like you forever!" He laughed. Before he opened the door he put his finger to his lips to silence her. He could hear walking and he stepped out into the hall. "I was just on my way to get you Sir. The King can't find his bride and is asking for her." the messenger said. "She is probably still trying to find her way around the castle" Nivek said laughed casually. "Come I will help you look for her." As they left in a different direction, Jezebel made her way back to her room to clean up.

She was so happy to have been with the love of her life.

"So that is what love is all about" she thought to herself. "That was a glorious experience. No wonder Ahab wants to feel like that all the time." She noticed Ahab almost always felt physically drained after sex but she felt empowered...that was something to consider too. A knock came at the door and a servant girl asked if she was alright and to announce that dinner was served. She laughed and said "I am wonderful. Tell my husband I will be there shortly."

A consequence for every action

The affair between Nivek and Jezebel had been going about 8 months before doctors announced she was pregnant. She spent equal time between her husband and her lover, so it was one or the other that sired the child. She was so hopeful that the child belonged to Nivek. A living breathing reminder of their love would be so amazing. If it was a boy, she would give him the Kingdom. Their Son would be King, and if turned out to be Ahab's son, well then, he would inherit the kingdom as well. It seemed like a win or win situation for Jezebel.

Nivek was not thrilled at the news. "I don't know what to say." he said as he ran his hand through this hair and over his face. Throughout all of the dangerous affair he had never considered this might happened. He thought his method of not spilling his seed in her was a fool proof way of not impregnating her. "Is it possible it is Ahab's child?" he asked.

"Yes of course it's possible" Jezebel pouted. "But wouldn't it be wonderful if it is yours? Ours? A symbol of our love?"

He grabbed her shoulders and said "Jezebel you are Queen, married to the King! This could be death for me if the King even suspected that was my child!"

Jezebel ferociously responded to him "Never! I would gladly cut his throat in front of his own court to spare even an insult to your name!"

He held her against him tightly, so she could not see the fear in his eyes. The fantasy had suddenly been replaced by reality. And reality can be harsh sometimes.

That evening the King was informed of the pregnancy and he was extremely happy! He had the royal horns sounded and the announcement was made at dinner. A huge party ensued until the Queen announced she was tired and they retired.

The pregnancy was a difficult one. She was a tiny woman so as the baby grew larger, she grew more miserable. Jezebel had many tantrums and was very uncomfortable during most of the pregnancy. She would try to maintain her composure when Nivek was around but she was missing his touch and kisses. He couldn't be with her romantically during this time. There was no time to steal kisses or make love, not to mention the larger she got, the less desirable she was. He tried to be sympathetic but she was so sharp and hateful with her words that he didn't come around too much. This angered her even more.

He was used to his wife's body getting all contorted and misshaped but it offended him to see Jezebel's perfect body so stretched. Her tiny little feet were swollen so that you couldn't even see her ankles. Lust was the furthest thing from his mind. There was nothing desirable about her.

He had to be kind and show his respect about once a week but that was all he could manage. Thank goodness she was always surrounded by people.

He saw a temperament to Jezebel he had never seen before and it broke his heart. He had believed her to be so kind and thoughtful, never one to hurt another. Then he walked in her room unannounced, as she was in full tantrum. He witnessed her attack her female servant, striking her in the face over and over, then smashing food in the face of the servant. He backed out of the room and called for more servants to enter and assist the female servant. Later he asked Jezebel about it and she said the servant had brought her cold food. She was curious about how much he had witnessed but he remained aloof stating that he had heard something about a servant not pleasing her.

Ahab tried to be supportive but he always had a look of such fear and sympathy for her that it made Jezebel want to slap his face for just looking at her! "Men are halfway responsible for the pregnancy but they suffer none of the uncomfortable feelings" she pouted.

Later in the week, while she waddled to the dining room, Jezebel witnessed 2 lovers in the shadows, she stopped and watched briefly wishing she was the one getting all that love and attention. The man was kissing the servant so passionately and it was beautiful to watch.

He took his hands and held her face and pulled her back to look deep into her eyes...then it was as if lightning had struck. Jezebel recognized that move, suddenly recognized his form in the dark and she hoarsely called out "Stop! "The man dropped the servant girl and ran away to the dining room. The servant girl cried out "Your Highness. I..." Jezebel cut her off and said, "Do you service all the men or just the married ones?" "No ma'am it is not like that at all. I have never known a man." Jezebel laughed a little and growled "Get your things and get out of this castle. Or I will have you executed."

Under her breath she whispered "And Nivek, I will deal with you later."

Several days later Nikev arrived in her room with flowers. She pretended as if the events of earlier had not happened. It was in her mind to make him pay dearly once she had the baby. Thankfully again there was a room of people in attendance so Nikev was safe from discussing anything. He smiled his beautiful smile, kissed her hand, and inquired of the Queen's health and she smiled back and told him she was feeling marvelous!

When the child was born, he was the very image of Nivek. King Ahab was strutting around like a Peacock, so proud of his Son, but in reality, it was Nivek's son and the Queen knew it. Nivek tried to make himself scarce after the incident with the servant girl; especially after he had a glimpse of the baby. The black curls were flowing and his grey eyes were the same as Nivek's. A fear and panic rose in Nivek that he had never known.

The first few months after the baby came he was nowhere to be found. When Jezebel asked about where Nivek was, the King said he was away on business for him.

Both the Queen and King seemed mesmerized with the baby and played with him constantly. Jezebel was sure Nivek would have a huge apology for her and come back to resume their lives and love together. Perhaps even make more babies. She had rationalized that while women are big and pregnant men still have their needs so she would forgive him for kissing the servant girl.

It bothered Jezebel a little that the baby's father went away on business while he was so little but she just brushed it off her heart. "He has to go where the King sends him. Business always seems to come first with men, besides maybe there is a war that he is trying to keep from breaking out. I am sure it would have to be something important for him to stay away from us" she thought aloud to the cooing baby.

"You look just like your father sweet baby. You will be strong and devoted just as he is. Together we three shall reign!"

After several months, Jezebel began to inquire more about Nivek. She went looking and found that his room at the castle was completely cleaned out! Nothing remained.

Noone admitted that they knew where he was at. While King Ahab was in a meeting, she had the guards bring the travel cart.

She instructed them to take her to Sir Nivek's home to visit his wife. They took her there straight away. She pretended not to notice the look they gave each other.

It was a long quiet ride but once they reached the residence, there was a deafening, solemn attitude among the guards. They helped Queen Jezebel down from the travel cart.

She nearly fainted once she saw the tall, growing grass and then the abandoned house. No sounds were coming from the barn area either.

"Are you positive this is the residence of Sir Nivek?" she asked. The guards nodded their heads yes. She walked towards the house and peered into the windows of the empty house. The house had probably been empty for months and months. Walking back towards the travel cart, she told the guards to "burn it, burn it all down." She watched as they torched the buildings as she requested.

She was in shock as it sunk into her head. She then realized he had run away from her, from their love child, from the love they had. He had left them. One tear rolled down her cheek and she caught it with her tongue. The taste of salt reminded her that she was not a dead woman standing there, abandoned, thrown away. She was Queen and this day would mark the very beginning of her reign. She turned back toward the travel cart and ordered the driver to take her home.

Once back at the Castle, she marched into the King's bedroom. "Where is Nivek?" The King smiled and said "He has taken an early retirement, my dear. He and his family relocated!" Jezebel did not smile. "You old fool. He probably set us up to be taken by enemies. Loyal men don't just leave!"

"My dearest. His wife was ill after the birth of their last daughter and needed his constant help. I couldn't begrudge him taking his leave to assist her with an ill child! Nor to go far away to see his mother who was in failing health. Sometimes a man has done his service and earned his right to retire. Nivek was a great man, a loyal friend. I could deny him nothing." the King pleaded with her.

Ahab tried to hand the baby to Jezebel and she refused him. She opened the door and screamed for the nurse who was taking care of him. "Pack up that baby and all of his belongings and move him away from me. I do not want to see him or hear him crying. If I do, you will suffer the consequences!" the nurse ran as fast as she could because it terrified her to see the Queen in such a rage.

The King was shocked and tried to reason with her but she shook her head no and held up her hand to stop him. "Ahab, I want another child. A girl child. I want the nurse to raise the boy. I am not good with children period but I need to have more children, even if the nurses raise them all. Come with me now husband, comfort me." he followed behind her to her room.

After they had sex, she told him that she was missing her idols. "I need a place to worship my gods. There are no temples here for me and my beliefs! Only knowledge of your God. Everything is about you and what your people believe. I am a foreigner in my own country! Please can I have some temples? I don't even have any alters to present sacrifices to my gods! No wonder I am so miserable. It is so unfair that I can not worship as I believe." she began to fake sob a little and he hushed her by stroking her hair, "Anything you want my dear. Anything, just please don't cry!" "And I am not happy with some of the staff. They treat me badly when you are not around. They stare at me and some even laugh at me if I say the wrong thing. I am the Queen, wife of the King. I should have their respect!" "I agree my dear. Do you want me to speak to them?" "No, I want to hire my own staff to come in here and them do as I desire!" she said poutingly. Her eyes began to water, and he caved in, "Okay my dear. Hire new staff. I just want you to be happy."

Jezebel felt good that her plans were off to a good start. She just needed to make the changes that would push her into her new reign.

Hell unleashed its hounds for the next 3 months. Jezebel hired all new servants and fired all the others. The poor servants were devastated. Some had been lifelong, loyal servants to Ahab and his family before him. Ahab paid them all a handsome severance pays and expressed his good wishes and appreciation to all of them. Jezebel sat there like she had a mouth full of dung, making an ugly face as each of them bowed before her saying goodbye. Each of them pitied the King that would be left with this monstrous woman.

The next new nurse that took over the raising of the baby was not a very maternal type of woman. Her mothering instincts were not good. Twice King Ahab walked in and heard her talking roughly to the child. The first time she had told him he was mistaken that she was talking to herself, the second time he discovered her screaming "Shut up!" and snatching the child up from his bed.

Ahab gently took the child from her and then called for the guards right outside the door. The King was so furious he could barely speak...

"Get her out of my sight. Put her in prison. Do we have a prison?" The guards drug her away and put her in chains in the dungeon. Ahab stayed with the child that night and hired a new nurse in the morning. He made sure to visit the child several times a day to ensure his safety and happiness. Jezebel was still adamant that she wanted nothing to do with the baby boy but was please when she discovered she was pregnant again. She knew this baby was Ahab's and rightful heir to the throne.

Jezebel began to take an active role in the running of the kingdom. Her father sent the men that had volunteered to come and construct temples and alters. They were built all over the country, in honor of Ba'al, much to the displeasure of the masses.

Jezebel's father King Ethbaal came to visit. Once he saw his first grandson even, he knew that Ahab was not the father and that Nivek was the father, no doubt. The baby boy was the absolute image of his real father. He tried to talk Ahab into letting him take the child back home with him but Ahab staunchly refused saying "This is my son. I do not know why my wife has such disdain for the child. He is a very good child, but she has no love for him. I will stand beside him and raise him to be a good man, like his father."

The two men exchanged a knowing look but no more words were spoken.

King Ethbaal did not chastise his daughter for her radical behavior because he observed she had grown powerful in a short time. He asked to see her privately and she obliged him ready for an argument.

"I just came here to see you are well. I have some news that you should be aware of, 'our friend' that was staying in the country has escaped. I don't know how it happened. I have executed the caregivers and sent out search parties but there is no sign of her at all. I am sure you are safe here in your own country. I have done all I can do but she is gone. I am bound by my own words, I cannot announce she has been kidnapped or escaped as I told your husband she was dead. I waited to hear from her uncles but no word so far." He looked at Jezebel with a pitiful look but she had no advice for him only silence. Jezebel looked at her Father. He seemed so old and frail. It sickened her to see him so sick with fear. She didn't say anything, she just looked at him with indifference. Her father thought that maybe Jezebel just did not know what to say. The entire statement he made to her embarrassed and sickened him at the same time. Feeling it was time to leave, he excused himself and immediately left the castle, headed home. Jezebel did not care, not one little bit. Didn't her Father understand she had so much else on her mind? Other important things, not the fate of a woman she barely knew; she had quite the fight on her hands trying to convert all the countrymen to her religion and fighting the believers of the true God. Men were prophesying her death! War was always an issue to be reckoned with...not run away women.

Jezebel let it be known throughout the land that the worship of Ba'al was the chosen religion in her land and the people had better get used to it. There was upheaval everywhere within the country but Jezebel was determined to stand her ground and convert the masses. The Army when they were home, was inflated to handle the discord with the people. Word was sent to all that the new Queen worshipped Ba'al and encouraged all to follow her. King Ahab was too afraid of upsetting her to argue one bit. Even his closest advisors were terrified to oppose his wife. The fits she threw usually ended up with someone being fired or worse executed. She had several hangman's towers erected in the town square and hand-picked examples of traitors and had them publicly hanged.

There were believers of the true God who were still in the country and Jezebel was trying hard to push them out of the country or eliminate them altogether.

She had attempted to softly convert the masses to her religion at first but ended up using a heavy hand to convince them to see things her way. If anyone came to the King for help, the condition Jezebel put on the help was their conversion and sacrifices made to Ba'al. When the draught came to their area, the fields were drying up, crops were dying from lack of rain, and animals were dying from lack of water. Jezebel widely encouraged women to sacrifice their babies in fire to her god Ba'al and promised he would bring rain. After all, he was a god of nature!

In desperation many women did it voluntarily or their farmer husbands abducted the children and sacrificed them without their mother's knowledge. There was great horror and grief among the masses. Mothers wailing was as common as crickets chirping at night.

Of course, it did not help her mental state at all that Elijah had prophesied that his God would not let it rain for 3 years.

Jezebel was a dark, evil woman who had no kind thoughts for anyone but herself and her empowerment. If the King opposed her, she threatened to sacrifice the children already born to them, and the one she was carrying; just to convince the King to let her have her way. He spent all the time of their childhood trying to protect his own children from their mother.

Each time she became pregnant he had a heavy heart knowing the mental strain that was to come to him. She always used the children as tools against him. He had them under constant guard to make sure she did not make good on her threat to sacrifice them to her god Ba'al. King Ahab even served Ba'al just to keep an eye on his wife and her actions both good and evil.

Jezebel was a convincing woman with absolutely no negotiation skills. Whatever the situation, it had to be her way or no way at all. He did not see this as he was courting her. He could only feel the electric shock that she made pour through his heart every time she looked at him. He was scared of her but still so much in love with her. All that she did or tried to do was for the good of his kingdom, it was just that her temperament was so harsh, her delivery so mean. She was not a good mother but he assumed most women of great wealth were not, so he did not slander her for that. Ahab had decided to take his life into his own hands and speak to her privately about taking some concubines. Jezebel was no longer interested in the beautiful act of lovemaking and well a man has needs. She would probably put a stipulation on the selection of women; He could hear her now possibly saying, "She has to be fat, or extremely ugly, or have a physical disability" Ugh that beastly woman sure can ruin a good thought for me" the King said with a sigh.

Final Chapter

One day while Jezebel was going over some papers, a servant came and presented a message that had been delivered for her. The note plainly said "I am alive and I wish to see you. I will send you instructions of where to meet me. I have never stopped loving you."

Jezebel felt a little sick to her stomach. How dare he contact her like this! Say these words over a note! He must be mad with grief over leaving her! She read it once more then ripped it up and fed it to the fire. As she watched it burn, she asked, "Did you read this note? Did you see the person that delivered this note?"

The servant said "No my Queen! It was left on the doorstep. I did not read it; Was I wrong to deliver it to you?"

"Don't be stupid. Of course, you did right bringing it to me! Should there shall be another note...alert everyone that if that note is read, someone will die. Do I make myself clear? As all of you know, I value my privacy."

The servant bowed and exclaimed, "I shall give a reminder to all, my Queen!"

The second note arrived in 2 days on a foggy morning. The servant brought it quickly to the Queen. The note said, "Meet me at dusk, in the west garden by the water fountain." Jezebel sat down. The servant asked if she was okay. She waved him away as she headed to the fire with the note, the servant bowed and left the room.

Thoughts were raging through her mind...both weakness and indignation were her first emotions. How dare he just show back up, after all of these years? What did he want? Her love? Her forgiveness?

Did he want to come back to his position with the King and just pick up where they left off? She thought she just needed to see him one more time. She needed to break his heart, the way he broke hers. She would tell him how she had abandoned their child just as he had abandoned their love. She would rub it in his face so that she would never hug or kiss that reminder of the feelings she had for him. She would let him know it was all his fault that she could not stand the sight of that child, that constant reminder of her failure in love.

Jezebel noticed she was drenched in sweat and her hands were trembling.

She went to her dressing room to look through her dresses. She would confront her past in one of her most lovely and expensive dresses. Just the sight of what he had left behind would make his heart explode. She held up dress after dress, throwing them each aside. Jezebel shook her head angrily thinking, "There is nothing here that screams revenge."

Jezebel decided on a sexy shift and slippers. She would be covered by a silk robe. The night clothes would torture him.

She didn't have much to say at dinner and excused herself early. The King assumed she must not feel well and wished her good health as she left the dining hall. King Ahab was relieved that she was not in her usual form, insulting and intimidating everyone. He had grown tired of making excuses for her long ago. So many times, he had wished he dared to take mistresses because he longed for a tender touch. He was just too weary of Jezebel's moods to even dream of kindness from her. She would never allow anything that brought him too much pleasure. He sighed and remembered a time when he thought they were in love. Then he rubbed his face with both hands as if trying to erase the memory.

Jezebel's heart was beating wildly as she slipped into the garden area. She told the guard to take the night off, she had just wanted a peaceful walk in the garden alone. He reluctantly left.

It seemed like an eternity as she waited by the fountain. The note did say to meet at dusk and the sun had set. Then she heard rustling from the hedges. Her heart was pounding so hard, that she could barely stand up.

The thought of seeing him again almost brought a smile to her face, then someone stepped out into the moonlight. It was not Nivek. It was her mother.

Jezebel was shocked but not afraid. She knew her mother instantly.

"I am at a loss of words," Jezebel stated. "Have you come here to do me harm?"

Her mother shook her head no and tears began to fall down her cheeks. She pressed her lips together for a moment; then spoke "I have rehearsed what I would say to you daughter, there is so much to explain."

Jezebel laughed and said "Everything was pretty much explained to me by my father. You went mad and tried to kill him. He had to protect me."

Her mother reached out for her but she recoiled from her touch.

"Daughter, if you would consider, you have but one side of the story. I could never harm you; I gave you life." Jezebel did not protest so she continued, "Yes, I did feel that I lost my mind after years and years of confinement but not before. I believed your father and me to be happy until my own father passed away. Then your father's feelings changed for me."

Jezebel told her she would not stand for her to speak ill of her father.

"That is not why I am here. I am here to share my side of the truth with you." Curiosity made Jezebel sit down near the fountain. She mumbled to her mother to continue. Her mother smiled and spoke softly, "You were a beautiful baby. However, your delivery was difficult and the physician said I probably would not be able to have another baby.

Shortly after your birth, my father, your grandfather died unexpectedly. We were very close. I was sad, and cried often for several weeks. I believe this to be normal behavior for a woman who was given the news I was given."

Jezebel shrugged and said, "I suppose so."

Her Mother looked at her and said "You look so much like my own Mother, Jezebel. Your Grandmother would have adored you if she had not died from fever before you were born." Jezebel began to bore with this conversation. Irritated she insists "Get on with your story."

"It's not a story Jezebel. It is the truth. When I received all of that bad news, I was so depressed. My heart hurt so deeply. Your father came to me for relations and I rejected him. He was furious and started to storm off; as he was leaving the room he said, 'I will find someone who would want me no matter how they were feeling!'

I was just too upset to think about relations at that moment. I ran at him and hit him in the back and chest several times, then scratched his face, he slapped mine over and over until I crumbled to the floor. I cannot remember who attacked who first exactly. It was not planned; it was all done in the heat of an argument. We both stopped; shocked at our own actions. I reminded him that he had told my father, he would never beat me, then I told him I was leaving immediately and taking you with me to the home of my uncle. The next thing I knew I was imprisoned.

He did not abuse me, but he isolated me except for the guards who would not speak to me and he took you from me, depriving me of the person I love most in the world. He at least would let me see you in the garden once a month. He told me if I ever cried out to you one time, that he would stop me from even seeing you from the window. Even the 3 times I was near you, I was not able to recognize or acknowledge you because of my fear. Did you ever wonder why he loved the garden so? It was his secret that he was allowing me to see you yet keeping us apart."

"We had a standing date monthly where we would dress in our finest and have lunch or a tea party," Jezebel said aloud to no one but herself. Then Jezebel peered at her mother. There was no doubt that she was who she said she was, they looked too much alike for her to be anyone else.

"So you are telling me that you didn't try to kill him?"

"No, I couldn't kill anyone, it's not in my nature." her mother said softly.

Jezebel could see her mother wasn't scared or even intimidated by the situation so she asked, "Why do you think he kept you imprisoned for so long?"

"The situation got out of hand. He probably meant to let me go at first but time went by and his pride was strong. Each time he asked if I would still leave him I said yes."

"So you escaped from the house in the country, and found me, now what do you want?"

"I don't want anything from you, Jezebel. I only came to tell you why I was not able to be a real mother to you. I wanted you to know my side... Your father was the love of my life, he did not abuse me in my captivity except for depriving me of my daughter and my freedom."

Jezebel asked her why the chains hung from the ceiling. Her Mother smiled and said "I suppose they were there to frighten me when I first entered. However, no one ever chained me except when I was moved from the castle to the country house. I was, on the other hand, mistreated at the country house. The master of the house beat me several times when he had become drunk. A laborer helped me escape. He was a good man and could not tolerate my being beaten and... abused." She did not say raped but Jezebel could tell that is what she meant.

"Father executed all of the people at the country house because you escaped," Jezebel said casually. She didn't say it in a tone that would revenge her mother's abuse but it was said as if it were her mother's fault that all of those people were executed.

Her mother looked stricken with her daughter's tone with her but did not say anything.

"Did the master not fear father?" Jezebel asked. Her Mother shook her head no and said , "Your father did not come to check on me. He just made arrangements for the word to be sent to him that I was okay. I am sure he was afraid that one day you would find out that I was not crazy and he would be exposed for his lie. The country housemaster kept sending word that I was well and your father accepted that word. Since the King never came nor sent anyone to check on me, the master of the house probably continued receiving payments for my keep, even years after I fled. That is probably what got him killed. I have been free from there for years, I was in hiding from your father, and now I am living in another country, far away, as a free common woman."

"I don't remember you much. I remember hearing you scream at father. Why do I remember that?" Jezebel asked her quietly.

"In anger and pride, people sometimes react badly to each other. Your father loved to provoke me into anger. I would take his snide remarks and then I would blow up and scream at him. We both would say very ugly things to each other, only I usually said mine louder than most people. My own parents were passionate people, very loud when they spoke or argued. Shrieking is a trait I inherited from my father who had a loud voice, angry or not."

"Why did he imprison you?" Her Mother walked around a little way as if pondering the answer, "Daughter, your father is a great man, a man of power and pride. I think he thought he was teaching me a lesson, trying to get my attention and make me obey him. However, I was stubborn and angry at him. I told him if I ever got out; he would never see you are me again. He knew I meant it and was not willing to take the chance of losing either of us or his fortune. He even teased me at first and said he was giving me space to be sad. He came back about 5 different times to talk to me briefly, then he just stopped coming to me. My food was brought by the guards, and my immediate needs were met but my life was empty except for those moments seeing you in the garden."

There was a moment of silence then Jezebel asked, "Why did you wait to come to see me?"

"I knew your father would come here to warn you once he learned of my escape. I waited until he was back in his own kingdom. Then it was finally time for me to risk seeing you. I have missed you and loved you every day of your life, from the day you came from my body. I was held against my will, then I used my determination to save my own life. I wish with all my heart things had been different but they were not. I cannot change the past no more than I can change the color of my own eyes."

She asked Jezebel if she could hug her and Jezebel quickly said No.

Jezebel straightened her shoulders and pulled herself tall as if reminding herself that she was royalty. Her eyes were cold and her voice strong as she said, "I do not know you, nor do I know if your story is true. It truly doesn't matter either way. That past is the past and as you say cannot be changed. My father was good to me and gave me all he could. I have no feelings for you, as you are a dead stranger to me. Almost like a story character that I was aware of but not allowed to speak about. My young life probably wouldn't have been so fantastic if I had to share everything with you. But I don't hold you responsible for my feelings. If it's any consolation for you my father never remarried. Rumor has it he has filled the castle with concubines but no wife. He looks old and tired now and has a face of a man with many regrets. I don't hate you, again, I just don't have any feelings toward you. I am incapable of love; it is who I am. I feel that way about all people. I am utterly alone in this world. No mother, No father, No husband, No children, No love. No loyalty, nothing!"

Jezebel's mother was startled and started to speak but she stopped herself. She wanted to tell her daughter that life was what we made it and that she was so blessed to be Queen, so blessed to have her freedom for all her life and to have the privilege of being with her children. But she could see no words would turn her daughter to positive thinking. Her mind was made up that she had a miserable life and nothing or no one would change that.

If only Jezebel knew how hard it was to escape to a new life, to change from being royal to just being common, if her daughter knew how hard it is to live a normal life, maybe just maybe she could appreciate the life she has.

Her mother had heard terrible stories about Queen Jezebel being so mean and evil, and she suspected her kingdom did not have her best interest at heart. Otherwise, she would not have such easy access to her.

"I believe all that needed to be said has been said. I will take my leave now. I trust you can see yourself out?" Jezebel said mockingly. Her mother nodded and said "Take care, my daughter. I will always love you."

Jezebel held her head high and scoffed at her and said "Love is for fools and food," and walked back slowly to the entrance of the castle. She turned around to say to her mother that she would not tell her father that she had been there, but her mother was gone. Jezebel shook her head; she felt a headache coming on. What a night! Expecting one person, receiving another. Life was certainly interesting now and again.

Wars had broken out in several parts of the country. King Ahab sent thousands of troops and chariots into war and they emerged victorious. Jezebel insists the people double their offerings to Ba'al before and after the wars. Once to ask for his assistance in the battles, the other to celebrate their victories. There was a fierce battle on the home front too. Jezebel was desperately trying to rid all the prophets of Yahweh, the one true God as His followers called him.

A particular prophet named Elijah had "called Jezebel out" so to speak. He called her a prostitute, announced all of what he called her evil deeds, and spoke prophesy against her saying she was an evil woman and would die eaten by dogs. As Jezebel headed to her bedroom, she felt tired, drained even embarrassed that she thought it was Nivek that was coming to see her. "I guess that goes to show no one knows what tomorrow holds," she thought to herself as she entered her room.

Interesting Post Notes

Jezebel's husband King Ahab reigned for 22 years (871-852 BC)

King Ahab went to war with his Army. He was in disguise so that the enemy did not know he was there. He was killed by a stray arrow. His sons, Ahaziah and Jehoram followed in their Father's footsteps as Kings.

Jezebel met her demise when she met a man named Jehu; the then King of Israel. The one true God had commissioned him to rid Israel of King Ahab and all of his bloodline, including all priests of the pagan god Ba'al.

"And when Jehu king of Israel had come to Jezreel, Jezebel heard of it; and she put paint on her eyes and adorned her head, and sat and looked through a window. Then, as Jehu entered the gate she said, "Is it peace Zimri, murderer of your master?"

And Jehu looked up at the window, and said, "Who is on my side? Who?"

And two or three eunuchs looked out at him.

Then Jehu commanded, "Throw her down!" So they threw her down, and some of her blood spattered on the wall and on the horses, and he trampled her underfoot. And when Jehu had gone in, he ate and drank. Then he said, "Go now, see to this accursed woman, and bury her, for she was a king's daughter."

So they went to bury her, but they found no more of her than the skull and the feet and the palms of her hand. Therefore they came back and told him.

And Jehu said, "This is the word of the Lord, which HE spoke by his servant Elijah the Tishbite saying, 'On the plot of the ground at Jezreel dogs shall eat the flesh of Jezebel; And the corpse of Jezebel shall be as refuse on the surface of the field, in the plot at Jezreel, so that they shall not say, "Here lies Jezebel." ' "—2Kings 9:30-37

Jehu, the son of Jehoshaphat, was the tenth King of the northern kingdom of Israel. Jehu killed a lot of people. He killed the king of Israel, Joram, who was the son of Ahab, with an arrow through the heart. He also killed the king of Judah, Ahaziah. Joram and Ahaziah were related to each other through Ahab and Jezebel. In time, Jehu executed Ahab's entire family, including Jezebel, and fulfilled a prophecy of Elijah (1 Kings 21:17-24). Jehu also killed Ahab's friends and officials.

Aside from killing members of Ahab's family, who had encouraged the people to worship false idols, Jehu ordered his men to kill the priests of the pagan god, Baal, in a temple. He then converted the pagan temple into a public toilet.

Acknowledgments to, AboutBibleProphecy.com regarding King Jehu page 62.

Also by Lilly Buchanan

Bad girls
Jezebel
Rahab

King Marc 1
King Marc

Life in a small town
New Life in a Small Town

Standalone
Our Second Chance
Dannie
Leroy
Sugah
The Wright House
Jezebel2

About the Author

Lilly Buchanan is originally from Columbus, Georgia. She currently lives in Pascagoula, Mississippi. Lilly started writing when she was a little girl. Lilly loves pretty things, flowers, decorating, writing beautiful stories, volunteering and Jesus! Lilly has 2 amazing granddaughters, Jasmine and Alexandria. If you stop and ask she will show you pictures!!

About the Publisher

Self publishing with Draft to Digital has been an amazing experience.

9 798215 286326